FRANCIS SELORMEY was born near Keta on the coast
of Ghana in 1927. He was educated in Roman Catholic
primary schools as well as at St Augustine's College, Cape
Coast. He studied physical education in Ghana and
Germany and for seven years taught the subject at St
Francis Teacher Training College, Hohoe. Later, he
became Senior Regional Sports Organiser for the Ghana
Central Organisation of Sport and was for a time Head of
this Organisation. In time, however, he began to concentrate more and more on writing. His work included features
and script writing for the Ghana Film Corporation, and he
was responsible for the scripts of two films, *Towards a United
Nation* and *The Great Lake*.

Francis Selormy died in 1983 having spent the last years of
his life in farming.

D0147418

FRANCIS SELORMEY

The Narrow Path

HEINEMANN

Heinemann Educational Publishers
Halley Court, Jordan Hill, Oxford OX2 8EJ
A Division of Reed Educational & Professional Publishing Ltd

Heinemann: A Division of Reed Publishing (USA) Inc.
361 Hanover Street, Portsmouth, NH 03801-3912, USA

Heinemann Educational Books (Nigeria) Ltd
PMB 5205, Ibadan
Heinemann Educational Botswana (Publishers) (Pty) Ltd
PO Box 10103, Village Post Office, Gaborone, Botswana

FLORENCE   PRAGUE   MADRID   ATHENS
MELBOURNE   AUCKLAND   KUALA LUMPUR TOKYO
SINGAPORE   MEXICO CITY   CHICAGO   SAO PAULO
JOHANNESBURG   KAMPALA   NAIROBI

First published by Heinemann Educational Books Ltd
in the African Writers Series as AWS 27 in 1967
Reprinted 17 times
First published in this edition by Heinemann International in 1990

Series Editors:
Chinua Achebe 1962–1990
Adewale Maja-Pearce 1990–94

Series Consultant: Abdulrazak Gurnah 1994–97

British Library Cataloguing in Publication Data

Selormey, Francis
The narrow path
I. Title
823 [F]

ISBN 0-435-90580-5

Printed and bound in Great Britain by
Cox & Wyman Ltd, Reading, Berkshire

98   99   12   11   10   9   8   7

To my Father and Mother,
Felix and Patience,
and to the memory of Benedicta

The Narrow Path owes its existence to two great friends. I should like to say thank you to them for the encouragement and the guidance they gave me in writing this book.

F.S.

CHAPTER ONE

My Beginnings

My grandfather, Agbefia, was a wealthy fisherman. He owned four large drag-nets and three fishing boats. He did not employ people but he was the head of a fishing company. A group of men in the village where he lived helped him to cast his nets and to draw them in, and in return they received a proportion of the catch, which their wives sold in the market. But they had no shares in the nets or boats and were free to leave my grandfather whenever they liked.

Every morning, the old man would leave his house before dawn and walk on the sea-shore. He watched the changing colours of the sea and studied the movements of the clouds in the sky. From these he foretold what the weather would be like, and decided where and when to cast his nets that day. Many of his company slept on the beach, and when he had made his decision he would wake them, and give them their instructions before he returned to his house.

He was also the chief's linguist. He had to attend the

chief on all important occasions and to speak for him. My grandfather was a magnificent and awe-inspiring figure as, dressed in his hand-woven brightly coloured 'kente', with his golden linguist's staff in his hand, he conveyed to the people the wishes of their chief.

My grandmother, on the other hand, was not awe-inspiring at all. She was short and fat; her skin was the colour of bronze; she laughed easily, and she did her best to shield me, and all the children of the house, from the troubles that came our way. We called her 'Mamadze' which means 'Red grandmother' because of her colouring.

During my childhood, my grandfather had four wives, and between them they had twenty-five children. He had had, in all, eight wives, but the other four had proved unfaithful, or in some other way unsatisfactory, and he had sent them away.

My own grandmother, Yakuvi, was his favourite and the one who stayed with him to the end of his life. In middle age, my grandfather built a small, but strong and beautiful house, a few hundred yards away from the great family house and compound, which was by then teeming with his children and grandchildren. And he took only my grandmother Yakuvi with him, and together they spent the years of their old age in peace there. And during their last days, he married her for a second time in a Christian ceremony.

Yakuvi had eight children and my father, Nani, was her fourth son. He was the first of his family to go to school. He attended first a French primary school in Lome, and then a Roman Catholic school in Denu. He did well, and was one of the very few young men selected to attend the only Teacher Training College in the whole country. I remember a faded photograph that hung on the sitting-room wall during my childhood. It was of a group of students with my father, Nani, among them. He told me it was 'The Kitchen Committee', a group of students who organized the food. But it seems that they were not altogether efficient about it, because I also remember hearing my grandfather recall how he used to send a regular supply of food to my father in college. This food was shipped to Nani on a small boat that ploughed regularly between Keta and Accra because at that time there were few motor roads and few lorries. Inland travelling was done on foot and the paths were infested by highwaymen.

My father finished his training and obtained his Teachers' Certificate in 1926 and was appointed to teach in Keta Roman Catholic Primary School on a salary of £50 a year. It soon became apparent that he was a devoted and energetic teacher, but a firm believer in the use of the cane. His children were well behaved and worked hard, but later on, I was to discover, by experience, the price they paid for it in fear and pain.

It was not long, of course, before Nani's thoughts turned to marriage. He began to court a young lady teacher at the near-by Protestant school. She was untrained and so Nani was able to feel superior; but she was literate and spoke English, and so was a worthy bride for a go-ahead young teacher. Nani bought himself a bicycle and each evening he dismissed his children sharp at four o'clock and rode to the Protestant school where Edzi conveniently lingered over dismissing her class, and collecting up her belongings. Nani whistled the tune that they had agreed should be their signal and Edzi came out of her classroom and allowed Nani to escort her home.

It was not long before Agbefia and Yakuvi got to hear of their son's interest in the lady teacher, and they did not approve. This was not the way to go about things. Marriage was too serious a thing to be entered into on the whim of a young couple. It was a contract to be made, after earnest consideration and long discussion, between two families. Neither Agbefia nor Yakuvi was satisfied with their son's choice. Agbefia felt uneasily that, by sending his son to school and college, he had already opened the way to new and startling ideas. Aided and abetted by an educated wife, would not Nani become too bold in breaking away from the old ways and despising the old traditions? Yakuvi felt sure that a schoolteacher wife would not be content to serve and obey her husband as she should. She had had her eye for some time on a young relative of hers, a respectful and submissive girl, willing to learn all that Yakuvi could teach her about cooking and the care of children; a sturdy girl who would bear many healthy children and grow fat and placid. And now here was Nani insisting that he would marry this independent young lady, who earned her own money and spent no time in the kitchen, and even wore a European dress. Yakuvi also objected to the young lady's family. She felt they were too forceful and strong-minded to be comfortable in-laws for her son. Why, the girl's mother was a very independent woman, rich by her own trading, and she would certainly encourage her daughter to insist on her own way and would support her against Nani when the inevitable quarrels came along.

The disapproval was mutual. Edzi's mother, Dekpor,

4

regarded Nani's family as proud. They were old-established in this place, respected and conventional. Did they properly value the fact that they were getting a rare prize – an educated daughter-in-law?

But through all the discussions and disapproval, the young couple held fast to their intention. They would get married. They knew that their parents would give in sooner or later. Even when Dekpor said she would have no more to do with either of them, they were not seriously alarmed. If she had been absolutely determined, she would have performed the traditional gesture of tearing a handkerchief in two to symbolize the irrevocable separation. But she did no such thing. She only stormed at them and wept.

Edzi demonstrated the seriousness of her intentions by being baptized into the Roman Catholic Church, and after that the families gave in. The marriage was celebrated with all the traditional customs and blessed in the Catholic Church. Thus Nani, my father, and Edzi, my mother, came to be husband and wife.

At first, the young wife continued to teach but soon she retired because she was expecting a baby. This first child caused her much suffering. Her mother, Dekpor, came often from Lome to visit her and frequently urged that Edzi should return with her. But Nani refused to allow this, because Dekpor was a strong believer in witchcraft. She was convinced that witches were causing her daughter's sickness and Nani knew that once in Lome, Edzi would be taken for treatment to a fetish house. He no longer believed that all sickness was caused by witchcraft and he wished to bring up his family in the new ways. So he managed to resist his mother-in-law's entreaties.

The time for the arrival of the baby drew near. Edzi was far from well and the young couple had sleepless nights. Nani no longer found his work interesting and his cane was put to greater use than before. He worried a great deal about his wife, and often wondered, as the time drew near, whether he should not have allowed her mother to take care of her. After all, the old lady knew a lot more about these things than he did.

One day, as he rode home from school on his bicycle, his mind was so full of these thoughts that he rode into a little girl who was selling fried plantain. The child jumped out of his way, but slipped and fell and the tray fell from her hand, and the fried plantain was scattered on the sandy roadside. There were many people about at that time and soon a crowd had gathered. They began to taunt Nani and reproach him and make fun of him.

'Look at that! A teacher, an educated man, who thinks he is better than us! But he cannot look where he is going. He has learnt many strange things but he has forgotten to be calm and careful.' Embarrassed and ashamed, he quickly saw that the child was not injured, mounted his bicycle and rode off, more upset and worried than ever. 'I would have done better to listen to my parents,' he thought. 'This marriage has brought me nothing but trouble. But now it is done and somehow it must be a success. I cannot give them all the chance to say, "I told you so." ' And so, in two minds, he reached home only to find his young wife weeping with pain.

Meanwhile, news of Nani's accident had reached his father. It was an important day for the old fisherman and his company, for they were gathered together to perform a customary rite. The biggest net of all, the one

6

used for catching the horse-mackerel, was used only for four months in the year. For the rest of the time, it was housed in its own house and given the reverence due to a god. Before it was brought out of its house, a ceremony had to be performed in order to ensure a successful season, and this was the day set apart for it. The fetish priest had arrived at dawn, and found the household already astir, preparing a great feast. Four goats had been killed and dishes of all kinds were being prepared. The old man had laid in a worthy amount of drink in order to do homage to his gods, and to entertain his company.

Before the assembled company, the priest poured libation to the god of the great net. He took water and corn-flour in a calabash and holding it aloft he prayed, 'Oh, god of our grandfathers, god of success in fishing! Oh, You who are kept in a special house and regularly fed by our offerings, we are about to take out your net. We beseech you to collect all the horse-mackerel in the sea and put them into your net, so that we may continue to feed you.' He poured first the corn-flour and water on the ground to feed the friendly spirits. Then he took a glass of locally distilled gin and poured it out on the same spot with the words, 'Ours is peace. This strong drink is for the unfriendly spirits. Let them drink it and forget all their evil intentions against us. But if you drink it and get drunk, make war against those spirits that are our enemy.' The priest finally poured out some more corn-flour water on the same spot and said, 'Ours is peace. We wish all peace, success and long life but if anyone says we should not live, that one should remember that "Evil to him who evil thinks".'

Then the day was given over to feasting and it was

7

when this was at its height that the old man received news of Nani's misadventure. He sent another of his sons to find out exactly what had happened. By the time his brother reached the spot, Nani had ridden off, but the crowd was still there, speaking scornfully of Nani and comforting the weeping child. Nani's brother heard the whole story, paid the child for her ruined plantain and took her home to her parents. He then returned home and gave his father and brothers a full account of Nani's accident. The brothers were as scornful as the crowd had been.

'A clerk,' they grumbled. 'That is what he is. And all these clerks can do is read and write. They have no common sense.'

'He is too proud to look where he is going,' said one.

'He did not even take the child home and apologize to her parents,' said another.

'It is a waste of money to send children to school,' they all agreed. 'You see now, he does not even come here to pay homage to the god who will make money to replace what was spent on him.'

'And what about the ten shillings I have just paid that child for her wasted plantain?' one brother reminded them.

'We work and the clerks spend,' another summed it up.

The old man smiled quietly and said nothing. 'They are jealous of their brother,' he thought.

At home with his wife, Nani was, for once, delighted when his mother-in-law from Lome walked in. Dekpor looked at her weeping daughter and her distraught young son-in-law.

'Come, Nani,' she said, 'let me take this girl to Lome.'

8

Nani hesitated. 'I would have liked it,' he said, 'but I do not think it can be managed.'

'If it is the expense of chartering a lorry,' said Dekpor quickly, 'I will see to that.'

'Oh, no,' said Nani promptly, 'money is no problem.'

At that time, he had less than a pound in the world, but he relied on his family to make good his boast. Dekpor continued to press him.

'You really should allow me to take her,' she argued. 'You see, she is very near her time. There is no hospital here. If the birth is not straightforward, she will have to go to Lome in the end, and by then, it will be much worse for her. Or perhaps your parents will call in the old women of the neighbourhood to assist and they will beat her to drive the child out. And in the end, they will only kill her. You know what these old midwives do? They tell the girl to blow air into a bottle and believe that that will make her deliver the child easily. Be careful, Nani, that you do not lose my daughter and your own child by your stubbornness!'

Nani was frightened, and his mother-in-law's arguments convinced him. 'But, Madam,' he begged. 'Do not send her to a fetish house in Lome. Send her straight to hospital.'

At once, Dekpor prepared Edzi for the journey and hired a lorry. But just as Nani settled his young wife on the lorry, she had a convulsion. She rolled up her eyes and became unconscious. 'Is she alive?' cried Nani. Dekpor was not certain. She sent a neighbour for the nearest fetish priest and everyone waited impatiently for his arrival.

But the fetish priest could not be hurried. When he received Dekpor's request, he first consulted his god as to whether he should accept this case or not. He sat down cross-legged before the representation of his god – the bust of a mighty man, made of swish, with cowries for eyes, and white clay smeared over the head, and white calico soaked in palm-oil draped round. He poured an offering of palm-oil on the head of the god and recited incantations in a secret language which he had learned during his years of apprenticeship. Then he threw down before the god a rosary made of polished nuts of a particular tree and interpreted the way in which it fell. It told him that he should accept Edzi's case and so he hurried to the roadside where the lorry waited. Dekpor told him the story of her daughter's difficult pregnancy and the priest reassured her and said that all would be well. But when he saw the patient, still unconscious in the truck, he became alarmed and advised that she be taken to Lome without delay. He repeated his assurance that, according to his god, all would be well in the end, and demanded his fee, which was six shillings and sevenpence, a bottle of gin, and a white hen. For this, he promised to pray again for Edzi. Dekpor gave him a pound to cover the bottle of gin and the six and sevenpence, while Nani ran off to find a white hen. The priest did well that day, earning enough money to keep him for a fortnight.

Dekpor and her daughter drove away. As soon as they reached Lome, twenty miles away, Edzi was taken to a famous fetish shrine. She stayed there for two days. On the first day, she was given a herbal mixture to drink and was washed all over in very cold water in which larvae were breeding. A white fowl was used as a sponge. After this treatment, Edzi regained consciousness and felt better. On the second day, her labour began and Dekpor, remembering the insistence of her daughter's husband, took her to the French hospital. Here French nurses took charge and, although the labour was long and the birth difficult, Edzi was finally delivered of a healthy baby boy. The mother and child were kept in the hospital for a week before Dekpor was allowed to take them to her house.

News of the birth was sent to Nani. He was delighted that his wife was safe and his first child was a son and requested that they be sent home to him at once. Dekpor refused to allow them to go. Nani then wrote two very strong letters – one to his mother-in-law demanding the return of his wife and son; the other to Edzi saying that if she really loved him she would come in spite of her mother's insistence. Edzi was touched but quite unable to defy her mother. Also she felt the need of help in caring for her first child. She knew she would not get this help in Zomayi, where she and her husband lived alone at some distance from Nani's family house.

Nani set off at once to Lome to visit his wife and son. As soon as he arrived, his mother-in-law presented him with an account for all her expenses on behalf of his young family. Luckily, it was at the end of the month and Nani had just received his salary, so he paid part of the bill and promised to send the rest as soon as he returned home. One thing he insisted on; he wanted his baby baptized and this was done at once. The child already had a name. All children of his tribe were named according to the day on which they were born. This baby was Kofi because he had been born on a Friday. But at his baptism, he was given a Christian name of his father's choice.

The day after Nani left, Kofi became very sick. His

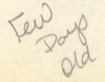

breathing was feeble, his skin hot and dry, and his pulse weak. His mother and grandmother feared for his life, and at one moment they thought that he was dead. On her mother's advice, Edzi put the baby into a large calabash basin and covered him up with the lid. She then took the dish upon her head and set out for a fetish shrine two and a half miles away. The rough ground cut her feet, and the bushes caught her cloth as she hurried past but she never stopped. She had to get her dead child quickly to a man who had the power to recapture life and put it back into him. She reached the place and threw herself before the priest, sobbing that her only child was dead and begging him to bring him back to life. The man hesitated.

'I am sent by my mother, Dekpor,' said Edzi. 'She says she will pay anything, anything at all, to have the child restored to life.'

The priest brightened. 'Oh, your mother is Dekpor,' he said. 'A good woman, a strong woman, a rich woman! Well, I must try to help you. Lift the lid off the calabash and let me see the child.'

Trembling, Edzi lifted the lid. The priest looked closely at the child. He detected the almost imperceptible signs of life, the slight rise and fall of the little chest, the fluttering pulse. The child was certainly alive. He straightened up. He replaced the lid, taking care to leave sufficient space at the side for air to enter. Then he said solemnly to Edzi, 'Your child is dead. But I will try my best to bring him back to life. Only, I warn you, you will have a lot to pay if I succeed.'

'We will pay anything,' repeated Edzi, 'to have this child brought back to life.'

The priest entered his house and prayed in a secret

language to his god for the health of this child. He returned and again removed the lid of the calabash. The child's breathing was stronger, his pulse firmer. He picked up the calabash. 'Where are you taking him?' cried Edzi.

'To the inner room of the shrine, where I alone may go,' he replied. 'A witch has taken his life from him, and I am taking him to my god to beg his life back for him again.'

'Will he live again?' sobbed poor Edzi.

'If God permits,' answered the priest.

He took the child into his secret room and in a loud voice he prayed so that those outside could hear him. He watched the child carefully as he returned to consciousness. Then he splashed the child with cold water. The fever subsided and the child screamed. The priest went out to Edzi and told her that the god had heard his petition, and the child was returning to life. But he warned her again that it was a difficult and expensive business.

He returned to his inner room again, and, at last, came out, carrying the child wrapped in a dirty white cloth. The mother gave a cry of joy and snatched the child from him and put him to her breast.

'You are wonderful! I thank you! I thank you!' she cried.

The priest advised her to stay with him for a week, but Edzi feared her husband's anger if he should come to visit her and find her in a fetish house. So the priest allowed her to return. He gave her a few simple rules to follow to preserve the health of her child.

'Keep the child wrapped in white cloth or wearing white dresses. Feed him only at your breast. Sleep in a room with the windows open, and before each window, put a dish of palm-oil. And then all the witches and wizards travelling about at night, who might wish to take the life of the child, will drink the oil and be satisfied and so will not enter the room to drink the child's blood.'

Edzi took careful note of all these rules and when she got home, she obeyed them.

A few days later, the priest visited them, and collected his fee of two guineas from a grateful grandmother. A feast was prepared for him; a whole fowl, a bowl of rice, and a bottle of wine. He asked if his rules were being kept.

'Everything is done as you directed,' answered Dekpor, 'and we sleep peacefully. You are indeed a wonderful man. All you say is true. Every morning, we find that the oil has gone and the child is undisturbed.'

Poor people! There were two dogs and a cat in that house and each evening, they happily fed themselves on three bottles of expensive palm-oil!

Nani visited his wife and son again. He heard about their visits to the fetish house and insisted again that they should return home. By this time, the child was well, the young mother more confident, and grandmother a little tired of the trouble and expense. Her daughter's presence prevented her from travelling and trading and funds were getting low. So all were agreed, and the following week a lorry was chartered and the family were received in Zomayi with great rejoicing.

No sooner had they settled down, however, than Kofi's sickness recurred. He was very hot and his breathing was difficult. No palm-oil had been put before the windows in Nani's house and Edzi knew that some travelling witch had got in and attempted to steal her

14

child's life. In her anguish, she rose up at dawn, took an old kerosene tin and a stick and beat the tin through the town. In a loud voice she cried, 'You witches and wizards of this place, leave my child. Give him back his life. Cease drinking his blood and I will give you good palm-oil to drink.'

'Is Edzi mad?' asked some who heard her, and Nani was ashamed. But when she returned to the house, the fever had left the child. His skin was cool and moist, he breathed easily and he slept peacefully.

From this time onwards, Kofi gradually grew stronger. His mother and father were proud and happy and lavished all their care and attention upon him. And so, in love and trust, I thrived.

CHAPTER TWO

My Early Recollections

I was introduced early to school. When I was four years old my father began taking me with him perched on the cross-bar of his bicycle. A sort of cubicle was made for me between the classroom cupboard and a wall. I was given sweets and playthings and expected to keep quiet in my corner. At recreation time, the children would play with me.

I can remember very clearly the day I went to school wearing shoes. In those days, even educated grown-ups who worked in offices did not often wear shoes, and it was almost unheard of to see a child in shoes. But my father had a friend who had a little boy of my age, and the two young men entered into a friendly rivalry, each trying to dress his child better than the other. It seems to me, looking back, that my father called his friend 'Cucumber'. I suppose this was a nickname. The child was called Koku because he was born on Wednesday. One day, the four of us set out to buy shoes for Koku and me. There was only one store in the town where shoes could be bought, and on the shelves there was only one pair of children's shoes – a small white canvas pair. At once, the two young men began to argue.

'I spoke first of buying shoes for Kofi,' said Nani. 'It was only when you heard me that you thought of getting some for Koku.'

'But I saw them first on the shelves,' protested Cucumber, 'I will have them first for Koku.'

The argument became heated and the storekeeper intervened. He offered to order a second pair of shoes from Accra. But that would take a month, so the argument about which child should have the available pair of shoes continued. The storekeeper grew tired of this wrangling in his shop and suddenly took a decision and sold the shoes to Cucumber. Cucumber handed over two and sixpence and began clumsily to put the shoes on an excited Koku. My father became grimly silent and I considered jumping on Koku and wresting the shoes away from him. But fate was on our side. The shoes were too tight for Koku. Cucumber tried to force his feet into them but the little boy cried and refused to walk in them.

My father's expression changed. He took the shoes and put them on my feet. They fitted me. My father gave his two and sixpence to Cucumber and home we went in triumph. My mother was delighted and I was excited. I was the only child in the town with shoes!

It was with difficulty that I was persuaded to take them off at bedtime, and when I woke in the middle of the night, I thought of them. I woke my mother. 'Where are my shoes?', I asked her, terrified that they had gone.

'In your father's room,' she answered. I climbed down

from the bed that I shared with my mother, took the hurricane lamp that was always kept burning to discourage evil spirits from entering our room, and went to my father. He sat up as soon as I entered.

'What do you want, little boy?' he asked.

'My shoes, Papa.'

He sank back, and I picked up my shoes and ran back to my mother's room. I slept the rest of the night with my shoes in my arms.

The next morning my mother had difficulty in getting my shoes off my feet long enough to bathe me. And at school, I was the hero of the hour. I insisted on getting down from my father's bicycle at the entrance to the school compound, and walking across the sand to the classroom block. The school-children clustered round me, except those that were afraid of my father. They hung back and hid in corners, but they watched me just the same.

At this time, I grew more and more troublesome and began to be impertinent. My father decided that it was time I was taken in hand, and in his opinion, it was necessary not to spare the rod in order not to spoil the child. This was a great source of quarrelling between my parents, and each time my father and mother quarrelled, I enjoyed it. Sometimes, I deliberately worked my mother up against my father and then went out, crying, to sit in the corner of the kitchen to enjoy the battle!

'What has he done?' my mother would cry, when she heard my howls and the heavy sound of my father slapping me.

'Look what he has done!' my father would answer, pointing to a broken cup on the floor.

'What is the good of slapping such a little boy so hard, just for breaking a cup? It was an accident,' my mother would say.

'It isn't for breaking the cup,' my father would shout. 'I don't care if he breaks everything in the house! It is because he is careless and thoughtless and rough. He has got to be checked.'

Sometimes, my mother would become partly convinced and it would seem that the trouble would be quickly over. Then I would cry louder than ever, throwing myself down on the earth floor of the kitchen, and rolling about as if I were in great agony of pain.

'Look at the boy!' my mother would cry. 'What have you done to him? Why do you treat him like this? I know what I suffered before he was born. When I was having sleepless nights and was almost dying, you slept soundly and went about quite happily!'

'Nonsense!' my father would say, biting his lips.

'Yes, it is true,' my mother continued. 'I suffered to get this child. Is all my suffering to be in vain? If you kill him, I shall be the loser. You call yourself a teacher! You are just a child-beater!'

All this would revive my father's anger, and occasionally these troubles ended with my father beating my mother. When things reached this stage, I was very sorry and became quiet at once. At these times, my mother was the one who suffered, but when words only were exchanged, my father was always the loser. When my father beat my mother, I would stand a safe distance away and abuse him.

'Look at that small boy,' my father would say. 'He abuses me – his father.'

And he would beat my mother harder because he

believed that she encouraged me to defy him. My mother's cries would summon the people from the surrounding houses, and they would intervene and stop the trouble. By this time, I had quite forgotten that it was I who had started all the quarrelling.

For some days after, I was not taken to school. I kept out of my father's way. My mother and father did not speak to each other. My father spent his time in the sitting-room, my mother and I in the kitchen. I never knew how these troubles got smoothed out but, one morning, my mother and father would start speaking to each other again. My mother, with a hard face, would throw a remark to my father. He would reply with a false smile. But soon all would be forgotten, and father, mother and son, would all come together again. Then my privilege of being taken to school would be restored.

'Are you not coming to school today?' my father would ask me.

'I am not bathed,' I would answer.

My father would call to my mother, look at his watch, remark that it was getting late, and ask that I should be quickly bathed.

My mother would hurry about with soap and water and towels while I hopped from one foot to another. I stood in a large enamel bowl while she washed me all over, beginning with my hair, from water in a bucket beside her. I directed operations. 'I want my hair parted in the middle,' I would say.

'It is parted in the middle,' she would reply, as she rubbed me dry, and dabbed me with powder. My father would help me dress in a khaki shirt, and shorts with shoulder straps, while my mother rushed to the kitchen to get our breakfast.

'Hurry up,' she would urge me. 'Your father is waiting.' And then, as I mixed up the food on my plate with my fingers, 'Be careful, don't soil your dress.'

So I would bolt down the mixture of beans and gari and palm-oil, and drink a lot of water from a calabash. Then, I would be swung on to the cross-bar of my father's bicycle and be driven off to school.

Sundays were quite different – days set apart. They were solemn and quiet.

We got up very early, bathed and put on our best clothes and went together to church. My mother always wore African dress. This was made from three two-yard pieces of brightly patterned cotton cloth. One piece was worn as a skirt from waist to ankles, tied round the waist with a strip of cloth or one of my father's old ties; one piece was sewn into a blouse; and the third was wound loosely round the middle of the body. It is this cloth which is used when mothers carry their babies on their backs.

My father wore, on feast days, a hand-woven kente, and on ordinary Sundays a printed cloth, draped round his body, leaving one shoulder bare. But when he was acting as interpreter to the priest, he put on full European attire – trousers, shirt and tie, jacket, socks and shoes. The priests were foreign – usually Dutch – so they could not preach in Ewe, the language of my people. They gave their sermons in English, and they were translated, sentence by sentence, into Ewe, by the teachers. My father was one of these interpreters.

I felt very proud when I saw my father, close to the priest, speaking to the crowded and attentive congregation.

In the church, all the women occupied the seats on

the left of the centre aisle, and the men those on the right. Each Sunday, as we reached the entrance to the church, my mother went to the left. I followed my father to the right, but when he went forward to interpret, I ran across to my mother in the women's section. I felt very uneasy with my mother among the women and girls and so as soon as my father returned to his seat, I ran to join him.

My father was also the choir-master. When his choir stood up to sing, I would stand in the front row, watching my father beat time.

'Your choir sang beautifully today, Efo,' my mother would say as soon as we reached home. My father would not say a word, but it was easy to see by his face that he was flattered.

Immediately we returned home from church, we would have our breakfast. Then my father needed a long period of quiet while he prepared his lessons for the following week. I would be sent out to play with other children and called in for a Sunday lunch of rice and stew. My father would sometimes come into the kitchen himself on Sunday afternoons, and make a delicious salad for the three of us. Then, he would hurry back to the sitting-room to finish his notes before dark.

Sunday evenings were his choir-practice times. He went to Benediction first and after that, he rehearsed his choir for about an hour. My mother and I did not like this time. I felt that we were unprotected without him, but my mother had quite another reason. Her main objection was that the choir was a mixed one.

'Had you any women in the choir today?' my mother would ask my father when he returned.

'Yes, I had,' he would usually answer.

'How many?'

'Oh, just a handful.'

'Was Helen there?'

'No!'

My mother would continue to ask if this or that woman had been present at the choir practice. Helen, of course, never missed any, and my mother knew this.

Why these questions were regularly asked and why Helen was always mentioned first, I had no idea. To me, they were just part of the Sunday routine, and I never went to bed until they had been asked and answered. I enjoyed Sundays very much.

CHAPTER THREE

The Fish Racket

From Monday to Friday, our lives were ruled by school. But Saturdays, like Sundays, were different. On Saturdays, I became the child and grandchild of fishermen.

We rose late. My father had a hasty wash, I just threw aside my night-cloth, and we went to my grandfather's house, about half a mile away. I ran immediately to my grandmother's kitchen, while my father went to greet his parents. Then he joined me in the kitchen and we were both given our breakfast. My father and I sat close together, facing each other, on low stools, with our plates on the ground between us. We had two plates each, one containing soup and the other containing 'abolo' – a piece of steamed corn-dough, about the consistency of warm, new bread. My father picked up his plate of soup and held it in his left hand. With his right hand, he broke off a piece of the 'abolo' from the plate on the swish floor at his feet, dipped it in the thick soup and put it in his mouth. I couldn't hold a plate of soup steadily in one hand so left both mine on the floor. Bending down I broke off the piece of 'abolo', dipped it in my soup and ate it as my father did. His hand went up and down, mine from left to right and up, and we sat in silence till our meal was finished.

After breakfast we went on to the beach. This was the great moment of my week. I can see it now: the sparkling, foam-tipped waves breaking on the sand, and the endless ocean beyond; the golden beach littered with coconut branches, rejected fish, and all the odds and ends belonging to boats and fishermen. Here and there sat groups of men in the shades of the coconut trees mending their nets. My father greeted them and we passed. In the shallow sea, and on the edge of the shore, fishermen were pulling in their nets. If my grandfather's net was cast, my father joined his company and helped to drag it out. When that was done, he would help other companies in which his friends were working. As each catch was landed on the beach, all those who had helped were given some fish, more or less according to the size of the catch, by the master of the company.

My father always gave his share of the fish to me to guard while he went to help another company. At first, I sat there, patiently and proudly guarding the growing pile of fish. But then a group of my friends came by, laughing and playing. They called to me and I left my post to play with them for a few minutes, but always with frequent glances at my pile of fish, and with one eye on the figure of my father. If anyone came too near my fish, or if my father turned in my direction, I hurried back to my post. But the morning was long and hot and I was only five years old. I became tired, hungry and thirsty. Food-sellers went to and fro among the fishermen, with trays of tempting cakes, fruit and sweets upon their heads. I looked longingly at the food, but I had no money to buy things with. Then, one day, I made a discovery which was to lead me into such a tangled web of deception that I was in the end unable to extract myself from it. I discovered that the food-sellers would accept fish in payment for their wares.

I began by exchanging the smallest fish in my charge for an orange, or a piece of sugar-cane. Then, with a larger fish, I bought cakes and sweets and shared them with my friends. At last, the day came when, in a reckless burst of goodwill, or bid for popularity, I exchanged my whole pile of fish for food, and distributed it among all the children who came crowding round me.

During the next half-hour, while I waited for my father, I was in agony. At last, I saw him coming. 'Where are my fish?' he asked at once.

'I sent them to grandmother.'

My father was content with this answer. He took my hand and we walked to my grandmother's compound. There he spoke for a few minutes with his mother and then asked her, 'Where are my fish?'

My grandmother assumed that he was speaking about that part of the catch that was always put aside for him as a son of the house. She fetched a tray of fish and gave them to me to carry. My father assumed that the fish which I had bartered away were among those which his mother gave me. He was quite satisfied. He took my hand again and led me home. I could hardly believe my good fortune. I breathed easily again, and I began to think that I was rather clever.

The next Saturday, I did the same thing. I bartered away all my father's fish, I told him that I had given them to my grandmother to be put with those which she had for us, and I was not found out. I did it again the following Saturday, and again and again. But my luck was too good to last.

One day, everyone's catch was poor. The surf was rough and many companies had their nets torn, and so lost their catches and part of their nets. Nevertheless, my father collected a few fishes from those of his friends who were lucky and gave them to me to mind. As usual, I exchanged them for food. When all the nets were in, he came and asked, 'Where are my fish?'

'I sent them to my grandmother.' We walked to my grandmother's house and he asked her for his fish.

'Did you not hear?' my grandmother asked. 'Your father's net was broken. There was no catch today.'

'Yes, I heard,' replied Nani. 'It is very unfortunate. It will take a lot of money to get that net mended.'

'Oh, that does not worry me,' answered my grandmother. 'Papa must deal with that. My worry is what we are going to eat today.'

'Well,' said my father, 'I was lucky. I collected a few fish today. Shall I have them?'

'Where are they?'

'They were sent to you.'

'To me? No. Who sent them?'

I slid quietly away but I had not got far when I heard my father call, 'Kofi!'

'Papa.'

'Come here!' he ordered. I obeyed him slowly.

'Where are my fish?' he demanded.

I could give no answer. My father ordered me to reply to his question, and I could not. He raised his hand and swung it to strike me, but I ducked instinctively and he missed me. My grandmother screamed and began

27

to lecture my father on his harshness towards me. She said I would have collapsed if that hand had struck me, and perhaps I would, for I distinctly remember hearing the wind it raised whistle past my ear.

'You would kill your son for a few fish,' she cried. 'The child probably went away to play and forgot them, and other children stole them. Do not blame him. He is too small for such a great responsibility.'

'But he has always been responsible for my fish.'

'Has he?' my grandmother said, puzzled.

'Yes,' my father said, 'he takes charge of all the fish I collect on the beach, and sends them to you to join with the ones you give me.'

'No, I must tell you . . . ,' began grandmother. Then she stopped.

'Tell me what?' my father demanded.

'Leave this matter,' my grandmother said, firmly. She went to her big store and took out some dried fish and told my father and I to take them to my mother.

We set off home, and I thought by some miracle I had escaped again. But my father was not satisfied. He knew that both I and my grandmother were hiding something from him. He began to question me, and soon my lies were contradicting each other, and before we reached home, he knew the truth.

There was no help for me then. I was to be beaten. The special cane that was kept in my father's room was brought out and I was ordered to hold out my hand. He swung the cane up and brought it down with great force, but I drew back my hand before it fell and was not hit. My father was furious.

'If you do that again,' he said, 'I will beat you all over your body.'

I was terrified; too afraid to hold my hand steady and wait for the burning pain I already knew so well, and yet terrified of the consequences of not doing so. I cried and said repeatedly, 'Papa, I beg your pardon. I will not do it again.'

'You!' he cried, angrily. 'You will not do it again! How often have you said that? Hold out your hand!'

He raised the cane again. I was all fear. I could not move for terror. My father seemed to me enormous, his eyes shone red.

'Take it from me,' he said, 'if your hand is not out by the time I count three, I will beat you like a snake. And if you take your hand away again, know that . . .'

And then my grandmother came. She saw my father's cane raised and she heard his words and she took the situation in at a glance.

'Nani!' she called, dragging the name. 'Stop that! What are you doing to this child? He is a good boy, not half as troublesome as you were at his age. But you will turn him into a criminal by this treatment. He will become a miserable failure if you break his spirit like this. And one day, when you are angry like this, you will do him some lasting damage. Suppose your father had treated you like this, what would you think of him? Stop, Nani, and think. This is no way for a teacher to behave. Let this be the end!'

All the time my grandmother was speaking, the cane was slowly lowered until, by the time she had finished, it was held like a walking stick. My father turned away towards his room. I began to sob with relief. I was saved this time by my grandmother.

But the thought of my father's cane was enough to prevent me from ever bartering away his fishes again.

29

CHAPTER FOUR

My Sister is Born

Not long after the episode of my father's fish, my baby sister was born, and this event was the beginning of better days for me.

One evening, as we sat at supper, my mother said, 'I am not feeling very well.'

'What is the matter?' my father asked.

'Oh,' she sighed, 'I have been feeling bad all day.'

'Yes,' agreed my father. 'I can see that. Our supper tonight proves it. It has no taste in it. I only ate it to save a quarrel,' he added virtuously! My mother was not to be roused. 'You are right, Efo,' she said. Efo is a term of respect meaning literally 'brother', and it was the way in which my mother addressed my father at that time. 'I could not cook this evening,' she continued, 'so I told Anny to do it. I have spent most of the day in bed. My back aches so much.'

My father became more sympathetic. He called for hot water and a towel with which he applied warmth and massage to my mother's aching back and swollen stomach. He persuaded her to take some pap – a kind of thin gruel made from roasted corn – and finally settled her to rest on her bed. I lay down beside her, my father retired to his own room and soon we were all asleep.

Not for long, however. My mother's cry of pain awoke me and brought my father rushing in from his room. 'What is it?' he cried and my mother told her that the pains were terrible.

My father hurried off to call my grandmother, and I was left alone with my mother. The other members of our household, my mother's maid-servants and her young sister, and my father's young brother, were in another part of the compound and had not awoken. I felt unreal – not exactly afraid, but strange and bewildered. I did not know why my mother was in pain. I went and stood beside her bed and saw her writhing and biting her lips. I remembered that my father had made a towel warm in hot water and held it to her body. I asked her if I should do the same. She looked at me long and lovingly.

'Thank you, my dear son,' she said. 'But there is nothing you can do. Go to bed.'

I was hurt by her answer and went out into the compound. The moon was shining brightly. I felt the spirits around me. I remembered the words that I had heard from a missionary priest at a First Communion Mass. He had said, 'God hears the prayers of little children and loves to answer them. So the children should always remember to pray for their parents.' As I was thinking of this, my eyes fell on the bucket of water and the towel that my father had used earlier in the evening. I clasped my hands and prayed. 'Please God, as soon as I put this warm towel on my mother make her stop crying, and get up and feel quite well.' Absolutely certain that God would agree to my request, I walked firmly to the bucket of water and picked up the towel and plunged it in. The water was very cold. My heart fell, my faith in the missionary priests and their God was shaken. I dropped the towel into the cold water and went back to my mother's room. My mother was writhing in agony and did not notice me as I crept into a corner of her room.

Soon, my father came back with my grandmother. She began to take the cloths off my mother. My father noticed me and ordered me to go into his room and lie down on his bed. I went into his room but I hid myself behind the door and watched through the crack. I realized now that the baby, which I knew my mother carried within her body, was about to come out and I was curious to see how. But then I heard my grandmother telling my father to go quickly and fetch two other women who were experienced midwives, and I was afraid he might first come into his room, and so I went and lay down on my father's bed.

But I was wide awake. My whole body was trembling with curiosity and excitement and fear; my eyes were unnaturally bright, my ears unnaturally sharp. I heard my father run through the sitting-room, and out through the main door of the house, into the compound. I heard the gate of the compound unbolted and slammed again. From my mother's room, came my grandmother's voice murmuring words of encouragement and consolation.

'Do not worry, Edzi. Everything is as it should be. It will soon be over. Soon, you will have another beautiful child.' Her gentle voice droned on and on till it almost lulled me to sleep. Then, the great gate rattled and slammed again, and my father hurried back with two old women and they all went into my mother's bedroom. There was a short consultation in low voices; my mother began to cry again and then I heard footsteps hurry out into the compound. I knelt on my father's bed and looked out of the window.

There, in the middle of the compound, I could see a small hut and before it my father, my grandmother and one of the other women standing. Under this hut, I knew, were buried the tools of a powerful ancestor of mine, who had been a blacksmith. We were taught that his spirit lived permanently in this hut and from there he guided and protected his descendants. We called him 'Torgbui Zu,' which means 'Grandfather Anvil'. His house is still there and his spirit is still revered and consulted, petitioned and thanked. But now, his children have replaced his mud hut with a modern house of concrete blocks. Members of the family go to ask for good luck on all they have to do, and after a particular success, or in times of special needs, they put money and other gifts in the little house. I often saw my uncle throw in coins before they went off to fish, and when the catch was good, they made a present of the best fish in the net to Torgbui Zu. The bolder ones among the children sometimes crept into the little house, collected the money and bought sweets with it. We were told that children who picked up the spirit's good money would undoubtedly grow up to be thieves. Indeed, we had a cousin, Bensah – the third son – was his name, who regularly stole the spirit's presents and did grow up to be a thief. We firmly believed that the spirit had cursed him.

33

Now, on the night my sister was born, I saw my grandmother, my father and another woman standing before Torgbui Zu's house, and I knelt motionless on my father's bed watching and listening. My father bared his shoulders as a mark of respect and fastened his cloth round his waist. He held in his hand a calabash containing a mixture of corn-flour and water. He passed it to my grandmother who, in turn, passed it to the other woman. The woman stepped forward, stirred the calabash with her hand, then holding it with her two hands, she raised it to the east and to the west and began to pray aloud.

'Torgbui Zu, and all the family gods, behold us here before dawn this day, at the door of your house. Wake up and come to our aid! We are all as children groping in the darkness of this world. We are powerless and we need your help. The wife of your son, Nani, is labouring to deliver his child. We beg you therefore to go to the first home of the child, and to push it into this world. When we return to the house, let the child be quickly and easily born. You are the only one on whom we can rely. Prove now to us that your spirit does indeed live among us, and works for the welfare of those you have left behind. If you do not assist at the birth of your grandchildren, who will there be to feed you and remember you? Without your help at such times, your family would die out and be lost from the face of the earth. Torgbui Zu, you know more than we. Send this child quickly and easily.'

The prayer ended and the solution of corn-flour was poured out upon the ground. My grandmother looked carefully at the shape and the pattern that the white mixture made upon the earth, and she interpreted it to mean that Torgbui Zu had heard and accepted the prayer and would see that the child was safely and easily born.

The party went back into my mother's room and told her and her attendant that all was well, and she and the child would be safe.

For some time all was quiet and I silently praised my great ancestor who had taken away my mother's pain, when the God of the missionary priests had failed to help me. Then suddenly, she cried out again and I heard the women exhorting her, 'That is right! Do not stop! It is almost here! Now, again!'

I could not stay in bed. I crept out of the bedroom, along the veranda, and into the sitting-room. A few minutes later, my father entered the room. He looked at me, but he said nothing. Perhaps he did not see me. He sat silently in one of the arm-chairs.

The next moment, the cry of a baby ran through the house. My father leaped out of his chair and ran into my mother's bedroom. I began to follow him but he saw me and ordered me to return to his room. From there, I heard my mother ask, 'What is it?'

And my grandmother replied, 'A girl. A beautiful girl.'

'It is a big child,' one of the women remarked.

'And its lips are beautifully black,' the other added.

I crept to the doorway and was in time to see the cord cut with a piece of broken bottle. My father left the house, awoke a near-by storekeeper, and brought back to my mother a bottle of beer which he and the women insisted on her drinking. Then her attendants helped her walk to the bathroom, where they washed and dressed her.

Meanwhile, I watched my grandmother wrap the

baby in a cloth and lay her on a new mat on the floor. I crept into the room. My father looked up and smiled at me.

'There is your sister,' he said. Without a word, I lay down beside her.

'Be careful, Kofi,' my father warned. 'Do not disturb your little sister.'

I was filled with love for her. I wanted to hold her in my arms, I wanted to shield her from every harm, I wanted to touch her tiny hands. But I lay quiet and still beside her until my mother and her attendants returned in a slow procession. My mother sank back onto her bed which my grandmother had made clean for her. One of the other women picked up the baby and rubbed her all over with palm-oil, and wrapped her in a clean cloth and put her into my mother's arms.

This was my sister Ami. Her name was decided for her by the day on which she was born. Her name was Ami because she was born on a Saturday, just as my name is Kofi because I was born on a Friday.

The women went away. My grandmother prepared some breakfast for us all and then returned to her own house. My mother and the baby slept and my father led me away.

Every morning and evening, my grandmother came to attend to my mother and to bath the baby. She would lift the child from the bed by her two hands and ask, 'Are you well, little one?'

My mother would answer, 'She says she is feeling fine.'

Everyone was very happy.

When my grandmother took the baby, I would climb on to my old place on my mother's bed, and from there I watched my sister being bathed.

My grandmother called for warm water in a bucket, an enamel bowl, and the baby's toilet articles. She would then seat herself on a low stool, stretch her legs out over the enamel bowl, and roll her cloth up to her thighs and tuck it between her legs. A maid-servant would arrange a bucket of hot water at the grandmother's right hand, a bowl of cold water on her left, and hand her the baby. First, the old lady would bath the baby's head with hot water. Then she would direct that the cold water should be added to the hot until it was lukewarm. Next, with soapy hands, she would wash the baby all over, and rinse her well. The water which she splashed over the baby fell from the grandmother's thighs into the bowl beneath. The baby was not actually put into the water but she was thoroughly washed.

Still sitting in the same position, my grandmother would dry and powder the baby and rub shea-butter on to her joints to make them supple. When the baby was a few weeks old, my grandmother used a sponge made from beaten wood-pulp instead of her hands, and after the bath would splash cold water on the baby. This worried me because it made the baby cry out as if she were hurt.

The water which collected in the enamel bowl under my grandmother's legs was used to bathe me with. My grandmother insisted on this, because she said it would prevent me from being jealous of the baby.

I had good reason to be jealous of Ami. She took my place on my mother's bed and it seemed to me that my mother gave her all her attention. I now slept beside my father on his bed. At first I did not like this but soon I became used to it, and then pleased and proud to be there. With Ami's birth, it seemed to me that my father loved me. He beat me less often and less hard, and often he made me happy with kind remarks and little presents. Perhaps the new responsibility I felt as an elder brother made me behave better or perhaps now that my mother had a daughter, my father felt more that I was his son.

When he saw me sitting with my mother, and the baby, he would ask, 'Do you want to sit among women?' His voice made me feel that it was not right of me to want to be there, and when he said, 'Come and let us go for a walk,' I would get up at once and go with him.

The baby brought many visitors to our house. Most of them came with small presents – pieces of cloth, soap, baby's clothes, money or firewood. Those who had nothing to bring filled their buckets with water and carried it to the house. This was a most welcome present in a land where water was sometimes scarce and always had to be carried home.

On the eighth day after her birth, the baby, like every baby of her tribe, was 'outdoored'. At five o'clock in the morning, just before dawn on that day, my grandparents, my uncles and other relatives assembled before our ancestor's hut. Libation was poured by my grandfather and prayers were offered for his continued protection of the child and her family. The corn-flour solution was poured on the ground to feed the friendly spirits. Then a glass full of locally and illicitly-brewed gin – a strong drink called 'Akpeteshi' – was poured out, that the unfriendly spirits might drink it and become drunk and so forget any evil designs they might have had on the child.

The child was then brought out and laid on the bare ground under the eaves of the blacksmith's hut. A bucket of water was poured onto the thatch so that it dripped down onto the baby and made her scream. This was to symbolize the hardships of the world and to emphasize the need the child has for the care and protection of its family. One of the women in the group – also an Ami, a Saturday born – rushed forward and picked up the baby saying, 'Whose precious child is this? I have found it. Who will pay me for this child?' My mother then stepped out of her room for the first time and said 'I will.' She paid a token price of a penny and received her child back. The old women of the party accompanied her back into her room and instructed and advised her on the care of the baby and of her own health. She was told that she could then go out into the open air, but she must wear sandals on her feet, and a kerchief round her head or she would be attacked by the after birth sickness. She was forbidden to keep the baby out after six o'clock in the evening but she was advised to bring her out into the fresh air at dawn. It was said that the morning dew would make the child grow.

Meanwhile, the other members of the family and the guests assembled in the sitting-room, drinks were served and presents of money were given.

In the afternoon, Ami was baptized in the Catholic Church and given a Christian name. My father was happy that evening when all the ceremonies were accomplished. He called me to him and gave me a glass of beer.

'Drink, Kofi,' he said. 'This is children's day. I have a son and a daughter.' I drank the bitter drink eagerly to please my father, and soon I fell asleep.

The party continued. My mother's mother arrived from Lome, bringing with her many expensive presents. But Ami and I were fast asleep.

CHAPTER FIVE

My Early Education

When I was six, my father was transferred to the primary school in our own home town, and promoted to the position of headmaster. My mother's 'Efo' changed immediately to 'Master', and this was how he was addressed by everyone for the rest of his life.

It was decided that I should now begin my schooling officially, and my father directed the teacher of Class 1 to put my name on the register, and admit me into his class. The teacher pointed out to my father that I had already picked up most of what was taught in Class 1, and should therefore start in Class 2. My father was not in agreement with this idea. In those days, children did not start school at any particular age. They came when they could be spared from the farm or from fishing; or when a good harvest or a good fishing season provided money for their fees and books; or when the head of their family became convinced that schooling was a good thing; or when the child himself was old enough to beg his parents to send him to school; or could afford to maintain himself and, sometimes his wife and children! So the children in Class 2 were often thirteen or fourteen, and some were young men of sixteen or more.

I was by far the youngest child in the school, but the teacher insisted that I would be wasting my time in Class 1.

'Let us test his knowledge beside that of one of the best boys in Class 2,' said my father.

I and a boy of thirteen were called to the headmaster's office, and questions were put to us. The boy did far better than I.

'You see,' said my father. 'He should be in Class 1.' But still the teacher protested.

'No, that was not a fair test. That boy is an exceptionally bright one. And he is thirteen years old. Call a younger child of average ability.'

So a boy of ten was called, and this time I did better than he. So, rather reluctantly, my father gave in, and I was admitted into Class 2. That very day, my father bought all the books I would need, and wrote my name on all of them. My mother, on hearing that I was to go into Class 2, bought me a satchel. Every evening I filled it with my school books and carried it home. I had no homework, and could have left my books in my desk at school, as the other boys did, but I preferred to carry them to and fro, so that my satchel should be full.

I was very serious about school, but the strain ol sitting in my desk from eight to eleven, and from two to four every day, was sometimes very great. School in those days was reading, writing, arithmetic and religion. The lighter lessons now on the curriculum were not included then, and the methods and discipline were suited to boys of twelve rather than of six. But the class teacher was sympathetic. Sometimes I fell asleep at my desk and he did not wake me. Sometimes he sent me to run round the compound to rest my eyes and exercise my limbs. My father would sometimes teach me informally on our walks to and from the school, and in the evenings, and so I kept up with the rest of the class.

Another thing that helped me was my association with the missionary priests. In each mission station, the missionaries established schools, and the parish priest was the manager of the school. My hometown was the headquarters of the diocese, and as each new young priest arrived in the country, he was sent to our station for six months. Here he learnt the language of the people, and was expected to go out and meet them and win their confidence. He did this with the help of my father, the headmaster. The first question of each new priest was, 'Who is the headmaster? Take me to his house.'

In this way I met several of these young men, and they took an interest in me, and invited me to visit them at the Mission house. In those days the missionaries brought with them boxes of gifts – toys, trinkets, medals and dresses – which they distributed among the children.

I liked the white priests – not that there were African priests – at first for their gifts, but afterwards because of the interesting things they told me about. I learnt to speak to them in English, of some sort, as fast as they learnt to speak to me in Ewe, and this early knowledge of English was to be one of my chief assets. I also learnt elementary nature study and hygiene and other subjects not then taught in school. I even learnt a little Latin, for they taught me to serve at Mass.

Apart from these things, I became aware that there

were other ways and customs than our own, and this discovery started me thinking, and wondering, and asking questions. I also liked the priests' food, especially the roast meat and potatoes. But this had to be kept a secret from my father, as one of the strict rules of the house was that we must not accept food from other people.

About this time, another baby was born, this time a boy. He was born on a Thursday and was therefore called Yawo. A really beautiful boy he was.

The birth of this child was the easiest of the three. He gave his mother little pain, and his father no anxiety. From the very beginning, he seemed to me the best loved. His birth was marked by much expensive present-giving. On the third day, very early, just as the dawn was breaking, my grandmother arrived with many bundles and parcels. She brought two new buckets and a large enamel basin. They were all full of smaller articles and she unpacked them in my mother's room before my astonished eyes. There were lengths of new cloth, including a beautiful piece of handwoven kente; and all kinds of pretty toilet articles, brush, comb, sweetly smelling powder and soap, bottles of perfume, a sponge and many other things. In a ceremony that morning these things were presented to my mother. They were all for the new baby, and they had all been provided by my father. I was very jealous.

'Why has Papa given you all these things?' I asked my mother.

'Because it is our custom,' she explained. 'The father of the child should provide buckets for carrying water, and the basin in which to bath the baby. He should give everything the baby needs for his bath to make him clean and sweet smelling, and cloth for little dresses so that he looks smart. Then the baby must have a strong kente cloth in which the mother may carry him safely on her back. And the father too, must buy new clothes for the mother, for she sweats so much when she is pregnant that her old ones will be quite worn out.'

My mother glanced with a pleased expression at the new cloth lying on the table.

'This is a custom very much respected,' she told me, 'and a father who does not do it is not thought well of by his neighbours.'

'Then why did Papa not do it for me?' I asked quickly.

'You don't know whether he did it or not,' she rebuked me. But I was not to be diverted.

'Well, did he?' I persisted.

'No, he did not,' my mother admitted.

'And did he do it when Ami was born? I don't remember it.'

My mother shook her head.

'You are right,' she said softly, 'he didn't do it for either of you. I was very unhappy about it, and asked him many times. But now he has done it for Yawo, so all is well.'

This argument did not comfort me

'But why does he do it for Yawo when he would not do it for Ami and me? Is it that Yawo is a better baby? Does he like him best?

My mother tried to restore my confidence in my father's affection.

'Oh, little boy. Stop troubling me,' she said 'Your birth and Ami's were more difficult than Yawo's, and I had been sick. Papa spent all his money on medicine for me. Health comes even before customs, or perhaps I should have died.'

The thought of my mother being dead frightened me so much that I became silent.

But the belief remained with me, and was soon confirmed, that my father was indeed more proud of this child than of me. I felt that I was being pushed away. I lost the honour of sleeping with my father, for Ami came to take my place as Yawo took hers. I now slept on a mat on the floor of my mother's room. My mother was absorbed by the care of her two babies, born with a little more than a year between them. And my father treated me less like his son than like one of his schoolboys. The brief year of my closeness with him seemed to be over and Yawo became, and remained, his favourite child.

Our family, in the European sense, was now five in number. But in the African sense our family was much bigger. It is our custom to put into the care of a married couple young boys and girls to be trained. These boys and girls are not exactly servants, for they do not receive wages, and the whole household lives together as a family, but they do much of the work of the house and wait on the master and mistress. The master, in return, clothes and feeds them and provides them with everything they need, and the mistress teaches the girls the domestic skills. Many of the boys, and some of the girls, are sent to school by their masters. They return to their parents when their education is finished, and the boys are ready to earn their living, and the girls are ready for marriage. It often happens that a boy who, through the education and training provided by his master, reaches a good position, will take into his own

household one of the younger and poorer relations of
his old master, and so repay his debt.

My mother, at that time, had three young girls in
her care; her own young sister, a distant cousin of hers,
and a distant cousin of my father's. My father was
responsible for the upbringing of two of his young half-
brothers. All these children were in their early teens.

Financially, my father bore the burden of the whole
household, because my mother had stopped teaching
before I was born and had earned no money since. My
mother's sister, Anny, and my father's brothers, Tsokoe
and Akoena, were all attending school. They needed
books and fees and uniforms, as well as the food and
clothing that we all had to have. And now I joined their
number. My father's salary of £64 a year could not
stand the strain, and the family budget would not
balance.

Money was often the cause of domestic strife in our
house.

'What are all these people doing here?' my father
would say, when he came in from school and found
Devi and Tonyedzi, the two house-girls, sitting in the
kitchen doing nothing.

'Is their work just to eat and be clothed? How can
I alone provide for all these people without any help
from anyone?' he would ask my mother.

She felt that he was reproaching her because she did
not earn, and she would tell him angrily of all the other
ways in which she contributed to the upkeep of the
family and his own well-being. But the lack of money
was a burden to her too, and she hated having to go to
her husband and say, 'Master, I beg you, give me
money for . . . this or that.' Her demands, though

46

absolutely necessary, often roused my father's anger, and his words made my mother feel humiliated and bitter.

'I was independent before he came courting me. It was only in order to bear his children that I had to stop teaching. If he could not support me and his children, why did he marry me?' she asked.

So my mother decided to earn some money of her own again. She started to cook food to sell to the school children during the morning break.

Here, we do not eat early in the morning. We do as much of our work as we can while it is still cool, rising just before dawn. We rest and eat when the sun becomes very hot. Then we work again in the late afternoon and evening, and eat again when the work is done and it is dark. And so school-children carry water, and sweep the house before they come to school. During the morning break, they have their breakfast, usually some cold food brought from home, or something bought from food vendors.

My mother cooked large pots of nourishing food; rice and stew, or yakayake – a preparation of cassava, steamed cassava dough, rather like mashed potato – and spinach soup. At ten o'clock, when we came out of class, there she was, sitting in the compound, with the big food pots and a pile of clean enamel plates, unprotected from the tropical sun. For a penny, a child could get a good meal. Very soon, almost every child in the school was bringing a penny and buying from my mother. The parents of the children were delighted to hear that the food was prepared by an ex-teacher, who knew the importance of cleanliness. The children of our household, of course, got extra large helpings, and sometimes I came back to have my plate filled a second time.

Gradually, my mother's trading increased, till she was able to supply all her own needs, and to buy a much-needed dress, now and again, for the children of the house, without begging the money from my father.

I benefited most from her trading, for one of the first things she bought was a box for me. The box was not very large, but it was large enough to hold all my small possessions, and I was more than delighted with it. When I had put in it the few clothes I possessed, there was still plenty of room, and so I filled it with my treasures. Pieces of wood, shells and pebbles from the beach, pieces of seaweed, and even pieces of fish and slices of yam; all went in.

When visitors came, I boasted about my box, and invited them to come and see it. My parents were not pleased when the lid was proudly lifted and sticks, stones and pieces of fish came to view! But I was the envy of the house. Not even my Aunt Anny owned a box of her own.

The school-year followed the calendar-year, and so examinations and partings came in December. On the last day of term, we each took a cup to school, and were served with tea and 'agbelikaklo' – a hard round cake made of cassava-flour. When we had eaten and drunk, we gathered up our books and marched round the compound, singing.

We had two new songs to sing that year. One of them said:

'This is the harmattan,
The harmattan has come.

All the other seasons have come and gone
The harmattan is here at last.'

The other one said:
'Good-bye books, good-bye books,
And good-bye to you, Kofitse.
No more bending over.
Let us play, let us go,
Our holidays are here.'

We enjoyed singing these songs tremendously, especially the second. Kofitse was one of the teachers who agreed with my father that the cane was the cure for all boyish failings. His frequent command was 'Bend over!' We did not dare to sing about the headmaster, my father, even in the relaxed atmosphere of the last day of the school-year. But we sang about Kofitse, notwithstanding the fact that he caned someone who marched out of step! So, laughing and shouting, we dispersed to our homes.

CHAPTER SIX

Doing the Lord's work is a pleasure

A Change of Scene

A week after the holidays began, my father was summoned to the office of the General Manager of Schools. There he was informed that he was being transferred to Ho, as headmaster of the Catholic school there. Teachers employed by the Mission had absolutely no voice in the decision as to where they were to be posted. They would be sent anywhere in the diocese, and transferred at a moment's notice. This has always led to a lot of dissatisfaction, and been the cause of hardship and separation. Teachers were also transferred to other schools in the diocese as a punishment for reasons not made known to them. My father had only been headmaster of the Tegbi school for a couple of years, his family settled there, and his wife's trade was flourishing. It would mean a lot of inconvenience and financial loss to go. He was not pleased.

But the general manager was tactful and explained the position carefully.

'We are very pleased with your work here,' he told

Nani. 'We see that you understand how to rule with a firm hand; we see that you are conscientious and hard working. Above all we see that you give as much thought to the training of your children's characters, as you do to teaching them the three Rs. Your own little boy, now, we see how firmly you have set his feet upon the narrow path. You are the sort of man we need in Ho. There is a new school. It has only been opened a year. And now the headmaster, a really excellent man, has suddenly died – God rest his soul. What shall we do if we cannot find another strong man to take his place? The school is in a town where superstition and witchcraft abound. We may lose many young souls, my dear headmaster, if you let us down.'

The Reverend Manager paused. His words sank in. My father's resentment and annoyance died down, and was replaced by pride and enthusiasm.

'I shall not let you down,' he answered. 'When shall I go?'

The practical details were arranged; the date was fixed; the Reverend Manager agreed to pay the cost of transporting the family to Ho; and guaranteed suitable accommodation for my father

Nani came home to tell his family the news. At first we were all upset. Ho was an inland town, eighty-six miles away. None of us, except my father, had ever travelled so far. We were to leave our family and friends, to leave the sea and the shore, the lagoon and the coconut trees, and the fresh fish that formed the most valuable part of our diet. We felt lost and be-wildered. People said that the customs of the Ho people were different from our own, and that we would have difficulty in understanding and being understood, for, although we all spoke Ewe, we spoke a different dialect.

But my father's mind was full of enthusiasm for his new responsibility, and my young mind was full of excitement at the thought of the long journey and new faces and new adventures. So my mother soon cheered up and began to make plans. First we had to decide who was coming with us to Ho. My father's young brothers were both ready to enter the last class at school – Standard 7. But the Ho school only went up as far as Standard 3. So they certainly must stay behind in order to finish their education. My grandfather took them back into his care. In return, my father took into his household his nephew, Sika, my elder uncle's child. Sika was about ten years old. He now left his parents for the first time and began his training. My maternal grandmother also took Anny her young daughter, away from us, and kept her with her at Lome. Anny was now ready for marriage. The two distant relatives, whose position were really that of maid-servants, were withdrawn by their families, because they were afraid to send them into the unknown country so far away. For a few days, our household was strangely small. The cheerful chatter of the five adolescents, the big family meals, the quarrels and games, were all gone. My father had no one but myself to keep in order. My mother went around with a worried face, wondering if she could get suitable maid-servants in Ho, to help her with the house-work and the care of the babies. She hoped to start trading again when she reached Ho, so she would need a couple of big girls in the house. Two or three girls were offered to her by their parents, but they wanted to be paid for their services, not to be part of the household. My mother did not agree to this. Apart from the extra expense this arrangement would entail, it did not give my mother full control over the girls, and would undoubtedly make for difficulties and jealousies.

But then, in an unexpected way, the problem was solved. The mothers of Devi and Tonyedzi brought back their daughters, and said that they had changed their minds and would like their girls to accompany us to Ho. Apparently, when the girls returned to their homes, small villages in the bush, they were shocked and distressed at what they found there. Girls of their age went naked except for rows of beads around their hips and a strip of cloth between their legs. They spent the morning on the sea-shore bargaining for fish, carried it home and cleaned and smoked it. They were none too careful about their cleanliness and smelt always of fish, smoke and sweat. Devi and Tonyedzi were expected to make themselves useful in the same way and they were appalled. My mother had taught them to bath twice a day and to take care of their appearance. My father had provided them with enough clothes to be always decently and neatly dressed. They wept with shame and disgust when they saw their fellow villagers, and their mothers were appalled at the thought that they would have fine ladies on their hands to be waited on! So back they came to us to complete their training and to be assisted to marry suitable young men.

The great day came. The lorry that was to take us to Ho arrived and all our luggage was packed into it. My belongings were all put into my own box. None of the other children had a box. Ami and Yawo's things went into one of my mother's boxes; Sika and the two girls had all their possessions tied in a bundle. My mother's boxes were filled up with household articles, my father's with books and papers. He did not take his bicycle, his gun or some of his heavy furniture. My mother had with her enough cooked food to last the eight of us the whole day.

All was set by the middle of the morning. Affectionate farewells were taken of our grandparents and aunts and cousins. A group of my playfellows came to say good-bye, and I saw one of them weeping. At this sight, the full meaning of our parting came over me, and, although I was eager for the great adventure, I turned my head away and wept bitterly. But the lorry moved off, my friends faded into the distance, I dried my eyes and became exhilarated by the cool wind that blew in my face. My mother, with Yawo in her lap, and my father sat in the front with the driver. Behind, in the body of the lorry with all the luggage, were Ami and I in the care of Devi and Tonyedzi, and Sika who could take care of himself.

We drove on for many hours, with occasional stops to rest and stretch our legs and to eat and drink. The landscape changed. The sea and the coconut trees and the fishermen were left behind. We bumped and swayed along the earth road into the land of forest and cocoa farms. Every few miles, my father would turn round to look at us and make sure we were all right.

'Are you comfortable, Kofi?' 'Girls, are the children all right?' 'Sika, don't lean over the side.' 'Children, is there anything you need?' But there was nothing wrong. We gazed at the passing scenery till we were tired and then we slept, with the child's ability to sleep anywhere and wake refreshed.

We reached Ho at 5.30 in the evening, an hour before dark. A large crowd was gathered to meet us. We were

54

very welcome, for a headmaster in those days was more than just the senior teacher in a school. He was the leader of the literate community, and the man who brought not only book-learning, but often the knowledge of hygiene and the explanation of new ways, and he was the man who bridged the gap between the people and the missionaries and the government officials. The Christian and literate community was delighted to have a headmaster again.

We children were passed out of the lorry into willing and friendly hands. While my father and mother were being greeted and received, Ami and I were taken round the town to see and be seen. We heard the remarks of the people.

'Look, those are the children of the new headmaster.'

'How old do you think they are?'

'There is another one too, a baby boy.'

'How smart they look. See, the boy has shoes on.'

After about half an hour, we were returned to the lorry and found our parents anxiously awaiting us.

'Where are those children?' my father was saying. I was then some yards from the lorry and surrounded by children of my own age. I hoped my father would think I had been there all the time.

'I am here, Papa,' I called. But my father was never deceived by me!

'Where have you been?' he asked irritably.

'I have been to see the town. A man took me.'

'What can you see at this time of the night?' my father demanded.

'I have seen the school, and the church, and the Reverend Father's house,' I told him.

My father calmed down.

'Well,' he said, 'you can see a lot of all these for the rest of your life. After all, we have come here to stay. There is no reason for you to be in a hurry. Go into the house, Kofi, with your mother and the little ones, while the lorry is unloaded.'

I ran into the house and inspected every room. It was a rectangular-shaped house, made of swish and roofed with iron sheets. The short end of the house faced the road and the end room, very close to the road, was an empty store, furnished with a long counter and long shelves behind it. My mother was delighted. Here she would open a shop and earn her money and keep an eye on her household at the same time.

There were two bedrooms, a sitting-room, a kitchen and a veranda. A little way away from the house, was a bathroom and latrine. The main entrance to the house boasted a pair of stout double doors and there was a separate entrance to the shop.

While my father, Sika and the girls, the lorry driver and his mate, and some of our new friends unloaded our things, and I ran about exploring, my mother gave Yawo his supper of pap – (a thin porridge made from corn-dough). When I saw this, I realized how hungry I was and began to beg my mother for something to eat. She quickly got out her coal-pot and charcoal, and gave Devi some food to heat up for us all. My father and the lorry driver and his mate came in just then, the unloading finished, and we all gathered together to eat our first meal in our new home.

After this, we all felt sleepy. Yawo was quickly bathed and we all settled down to sleep. Father, mother and the three children occupied one bedroom. The mattresses from my parents' beds had been put down on the floor and we shared them. They were made of cocoa sacks and filled with straw. In the other room, the two girls and Sika slept on 'atsatsa', which are mats made of bundles of reeds tied together. My father offered the lorry driver and his mate the use of the veranda, so that they could put mats down and sleep there. But the lorry driver insisted that they should sleep in the lorry, for he did not trust the people of this unknown town and was afraid that some of the parts of the lorry might be stolen if it were left unguarded.

We all slept soundly that night because we were so tired. Even Yawo did not wake and cry. Everything was peaceful in our new house.

When we woke the next morning, we found that our new neighbours had already carried water for us, and had filled a forty-four-gallon drum that we had brought with us from Tegbi. My father rose first, bathed, dressed and went to report his arrival to his new manager, the parish priest, at the Mission house. Before he returned, we were all washed and dressed, and breakfast had been prepared by my mother. We all ate together again, and then my father paid the lorry driver, and the lorry set off back to Tegbi, and so we watched the last link with our old home vanish into the distance.

My father went off again to pay a courtesy call to the head Christian and to make the acquaintance of his colleagues and neighbours. The rest of the household spent the whole day unpacking and arranging our furniture and belongings.

There was a full week between our arrival at Ho and the beginning of the new school-year. We all spent it in getting to know the place and the people, and making plans for our life here. My mother spent a lot of time in the market, studying the local prices and finding out what things were in demand, and so getting ideas both about her trading and about the economical running of her household. My father was busy getting to know people and things connected with his work. And I was very busy roaming round the town and choosing the children who would be my playmates.

My base was the Roman Catholic Mission compound. For the whole week, I went to the Mission each morning after breakfast. There I met a number of children clad only in small dirty 'pietos' – brief pants – playing ball or running about. My appearance, in clean, starched, and pressed shirt and shorts always brought the game to an end. I asked them to take me to see their town. They took me to see the Ewe Presbyterian School – a place over three miles away – where our rivals, the Protestants, went to school. They showed me the old houses built by the Germans in the days when that part of this country was ruled from Berlin. They were big solidly-built houses, which were being used as the Presbyterian Middle School and their seminary. Then they took me to see the European residential area, where the British Colonial Government District Commissioner lived, with other Government officials. The District Commissioner, they told me, was a terrible man and I must run and hide if ever I had the misfortune to meet him.

The next place the children showed me was high in the hills to the north of the town. There I saw a little waterfall and learnt that this was the source of water for the whole town. The water was collected in an artificially constructed reservoir, again the work of the Germans, and then carried by a pipe-line to the stand-pipes in the

58

town. It was not doctored with any chemical but that did not worry me. I had never heard of the need for it. It seemed marvellous to me that all one had to do in order to get water was to turn on a tap. At home, fresh water was very precious.

But the most fascinating things of all to me, were the abundance of mango trees in the mountains, laden with the sweet golden fruit. The boys climbed up them like little monkeys and picked the mangoes and ate them. The juice stained their faces and ran down their chins and arms and chests. But the moment they had sucked one mango dry, they would throw down the stone and skin, and climb the tree for another one.

I was astonished and very worried when I saw this. At home, in Tegbi, the mango trees were guarded when the fruit was getting ripe, and if a child was caught even throwing stones at the tree, he would be beaten. There were many, many coconut trees along the shore, but each was the property of someone, and no one could pick the fruit without permission. And now I saw my new friends eating mango after mango without a backward glance. I was afraid.

'Are we allowed to eat these mangoes?' I asked my friends.

'Yes,' one answered as he slid down the tree with a large ripe fruit.

'Who allowed us?' I went on.

'Nobody,' he answered impatiently, as he buried his face in the mango.

I stood, miserable in my indecision and my nice clothes, unable to join in the fun. I was afraid that if I ate the mangoes, I would be taken to the chief, as would be done at home. Then my father would get to hear of it and I should be punished and confined to the house. I had noticed when we unpacked that my father had not forgotten to bring his cane to Ho.

'Let us not pick the mangoes,' I begged my new friends. 'Look, here are plenty lying on the ground. Let us eat only these.' But my friends only laughed at me, and would not stop. Each time I came home from what I regarded as a mango-stealing expedition, I was afraid. But nothing was ever said, and gradually I lost my fear, and was able to go happily into the mountains, and pick and eat the mangoes, and even bring some back for my little brother and sister.

CHAPTER SEVEN

Settling Down in Ho

And so the week passed and on the following Monday, Papa, Sika and I had to go to school. My father got up early and spent more time than usual on his dressing. He wore starched white shorts, shirt and jacket. The jacket was belted and had pockets with flaps. He wore knee-length socks and heavy shoes. To complete the picture, he wore a white sun helmet. It was obvious to us all that he was out to impress both teachers and children, and that he would start as firmly as he meant to go on.

After a light breakfast, he set out. My mother called to him to wait, and shouted to me to hurry. But things had changed. A small boy trailing beside him would spoil his entrance. 'No, let him come with Sika,' my father said. 'I have a lot to do before school opens. Kofi is old enough to go without me now.' And off he went with firm steps, and a ram-rod back, his cane swinging in his hand.

I followed later and went to see him in his office. He gave me a note and directed me to the Infants' department. The teacher to whom I was directed took me by the hand, and I followed him wherever he went. Soon I found myself standing with him and the other teachers, on the veranda of the infant school. Before us were the children in their lines.

The first day of the school year was a big day. All the children came to hear the results of their examinations held at the end of the year before. On these results depended their promotion to the next class. The children in front of me were lined up opposite the classes they had attended last year, and they waited breathlessly to hear whether they were to move up to the next class or not. The teacher began with Class 3. He called the name of each child and announced his examination marks and whether he was to be promoted. Those who had good results departed happily, their books under their arms. They were leaving the infant-school block and going to the junior school. They were going into Standard 1. Those who had done badly stood still with shame. Some of them began to weep. They were to repeat Class 3 and they were already big boys and girls. In fact, the children were even older than those at my previous school, and I was again the smallest.

The teachers then moved to Class 2 and announced their results. The children who had been successful left with the noise of joy. I began to feel the mental strain that these poor children were going through and to experience it myself. At the end of the previous year, I had not known that the last test was going to carry so much weight. I had no idea whether I had done well or badly, and I stood on the veranda imagining what my fate was to be, and how I could bear it if I were among those who were not promoted.

So it went on. Class 1 was dealt with in the same manner. At last all the good pupils were taken out and others left to repeat the various classes. Many of the unsuccessful pupils were crying.

My name, however, was not mentioned and I did not know what was going to happen.

One classroom was still almost empty. This was Class 1. Then the little children from the near-by kindergarten came marching up, and went joyfully into their new classroom. This was a great change for them. Their previous classroom was just a shelter, roofed with thatch, and enclosed by low mud walls. They would no longer have to take all the school furniture and equipment to be locked up safely every night, or carry their books and chalks to and fro because there was no place to leave them. But I felt very sorry for the big boys and girls who had to repeat Class 1, and those just starting school. They would find that the children who had been to the kindergarten already knew more than they.

As I stood and gazed at them, I heard my own name called. I was to go into Class 3. I found that Classes 2 and 3 shared one classroom and one teacher. I walked shyly into the room. It seemed to me very overcrowded and all the boys looked large and rough.

There was no work done for the next few days. The time was spent in buying books. All the text books and exercise books were bought at the Mission book shop. This was only a few minutes' walk for us, but other children walked many miles into the Central Station from their little village schools in the bush. Education was not easily acquired in those days. Some children brought their own money and bought their own books.

Others were accompanied by parents and guardians. Some had insufficient money and had to decide which of the prescribed books were most necessary and should be bought. There were frequent discussions between teachers and parents on the subject of fees. Many were able only to pay for a month at a time. Some pleaded a poor harvest or a family bereavement and asked for time to pay. Some arrived and were sent home again because they were unsuitably dressed. Although no lessons were given, the headmaster and the teachers were busy.

But I was lonely and miserable and bewildered. None of the children spoke to me or made any offer of friendship. I had no book-buying to do, because my father simply bought all my books himself and presented them to me. He had even written my name on the covers.

Every day, during the first week, new children arrived. They were children who, for one reason or another, could not come to school on the first day. Perhaps they had been sick; or had gone away during the holiday and not travelled back in good time; or whose uniform – khaki shorts and a white shirt – had not been sewn soon enough; or whose parents had had difficulty in finding the money for books and fees. Some of these boys noticed me and asked, 'Who is that?'

And a boy would answer in a warning tone, 'Be careful, that is the new headmaster's son.'

At last I knew why I was being shunned. I turned away with tears in my eyes. One or two of the bolder spirits came to speak to me, but I felt instinctively that they did so as an act of bravado, not really out of friendship, and I was not comforted.

I noticed that none of the children with whom I had

played and eaten mangoes, during the week before, were in school, and asked where they were. I was told, rather scornfully, that they were not schoolboys, but farm-children. I realized then why those children had stared at my neat clothing. But they had been friendly. My father had no authority over them. They were free as the birds. How I envied them!

I asked what the farm-children did all day.

'They go to the farms with their parents and work all day,' I was told.

'What do they eat? Only mangoes?' I asked.

'Oh, no!' my informant said. 'They have huts in their farms, and they keep yams and cassava and corn there. And they pick fresh pepper and tomatoes and mushrooms from their fields, whenever they want them.'

'How do they cook their food?' I asked.

'Their mothers keep a set of cooking pots, grinding stones and everything they need in the farm huts. They make a camp fire and put cassava and yams into the ashes to roast. Then the parents go to work and the children watch the fire. One of the girls will grind pepper and cut up tomatoes and onions and mushrooms and whatever else they have got. This makes a nice sauce to eat the roasted yam and cassava with. When the food is ready, the children call the grown-ups and they all rest and eat. Then they all go back to work on the farm. At dusk, they come home and bathe, and eat the big dinner that their grandmother or aunt had got ready for them.'

Oh, how I envied those children: their carefree, outdoor life. No examinations, no inspections, no cane. Even my companion looked a little wistful as he described the picnic to me. But it was no good my wishing. My father was the headmaster, and somehow I had to be a credit to him.

At the end of the week, when things were settling down, and the children had all arrived, and bought their books, a great blow fell on me. My class teacher called me and told me that my father had instructed him to put me back into Class 2. At first I could not believe it. I ran out of the classroom, weeping and ran home to my mother.

'If that is what Papa will do to me,' I sobbed, 'I will not go to school at all. What is the use of trying?'

My mother's face set hard. She dried my tears and said, 'Do not worry, my boy. As soon as your father comes in, I will have this matter out with him. You shall go into Class 3.' I was satisfied and sat quietly waiting for him.

At the end of the morning school, he returned to the house, to be greeted by a tearful small boy and a determined wife.

'Why have you put Kofi back into Class 2?' my mother demanded, as soon as he set foot in the house. 'I want him to finish his schooling as soon as possible, so that he can go on to some higher institution and come back and keep me in my old age. And you will not give him the chance. What have you found wrong with him? Is he lazy? Did he do badly in his examination? Give the boy his chance. I am sure you would not treat any other boy like this.' My mother's voice grew loud and shrill. My father simply walked past us, as if he had neither heard nor seen us. My mother continued to press him for an answer. At last, my father could not keep silent any longer.

'What is all this?' he demanded angrily. 'Just

66

remember you are not a teacher now, and do not interfere with school affairs. I am the headmaster, and I know what is best for the children in my school. Especially for my own son who also happens to be one of my schoolboys. It is a pity you do not ask why I have put him back into Class 2, before you start shouting at me about it.'

My mother was a little abashed.

'Why did you then?' she asked.

'The teacher came to my office,' my father explained, 'and told me that he considered Kofi too young to be taught with the boys in Class 3. You see, we have not only to consider the mental ability of the child, but also his stage of emotional development. As well as that point, the teacher told me that here they use a different syllabus and curriculum. Possibly, Kofi will find that he has not covered all the work done by these Class 3 children.'

My mother listened intently, obviously becoming convinced. My heart sank. Against my will, my father was almost convincing me. To be honest, I was very nervous of having to compete with those boys in Class 3.

'After all,' my father went on, 'he will only go back a year and he is very young. It is better that he should repeat Class 2 now, and go into Class 3 next year fully prepared, than struggle along with work too hard for him, and perhaps have to repeat Class 3 at the end of it. This way, there will be no shame or embarrassment for him.'

My father had been speaking quite gently for him, but now he hardened his voice again.

'However, you must have your own way. Go to the class-teacher, if you like, and protest. If you manage to convince him, I shall not interfere. Only do not come crying to me if he fails in the end. It will not be my fault.'

My mother spoke humbly, 'You are quite right, Master,' she said, and turning to me, 'you must trust your father, Kofi. He knows what is best for you.'

So, my rebellion cooled from a blaze to a smoulder. I went back to school in the afternoon. At least, I did not have to face the humiliation of leaving one classroom and entering the other. Since we had not been given our permanent places, or had any lessons, many of the boys did not really notice that I had been demoted. My books were quietly exchanged for Class 2 books and I had to be content. The school year began, and gradually my classmates forgot to avoid me – perhaps because they saw that I was not treated any more leniently than they by my father – and I became absorbed into the school.

My mother resumed her trading. She cooked food again, and brought it to the school compound at recreation time, with the same success. There was always a choice of two or three different foods, but I always had the same thing. Rice and stew was my favourite dish, and at that time, I could have eaten it three times a day. Later, it was to have such unpleasant associations for me that I do not eat it even now with any enjoyment.

My mother also opened her little shop. She bought goods in large quantities, on credit, at wholesale prices, then retailed them, and made a useful profit. She sold biscuits, sugar, sweets, corned beef, sardines, soap, candles, rice, kerosene and many other articles. The goods were displayed on a long table outside our house. Sometimes my mother or one of her maid-servants sat by the table serving people and greeting passers-by. But this was hardly necessary for, if no one was there, the customers would take what they wanted and leave the money on the table. When food was left unsold after the school recreation time, the big pots were stood by the table, and workers who had no one to cook for them would buy their midday meal. When all was sold, we the children would scrape the rice-crusts from the bottom of the rice-pot, and run our fingers round the inside of the stew-pot.

Our household had grown again. At different times a girl, and then a boy, from Ho were given to my parents to be trained. Then a little boy from Shiamlolo, a village about sixty miles away, joined us. He came because there was no good school near his home and his family had been persuaded that he could benefit from a good education. He did, eventually, reach the university. At that time, Bolo was an undersized little boy, as sharp as a needle. He spoke a different language from us, and his first task was to learn to make himself understood. He was a great favourite with my father and mother. Somehow, he had the knack of keeping out of trouble. All the new members of our household attended school, and we were all expected to help my mother with her trading in our free time. After all, it was her trade that bought our clothes and any little luxury that came our way, so it was to our advantage to help it prosper.

I was often stationed at the long table during my lunch-hour. At first, this amused me, but soon I got bored and often ran away to play. But I enjoyed selling my mother's wares in the market on market-days. This occurred every fifth day and was held about two hundred yards from our house. On those days, we had to spend the midday break at the market, and return there again at the close of afternoon school. If market-day fell on a Saturday or Sunday, we went to the market-place about ten o'clock in the morning and stayed there all day. I usually sold kerosene. I enjoyed the pouring and measuring and was often given a few pence to spend as I liked.

On other days, I spent my free time at the Mission house, as I had done at home. But now that I was older, I was expected to make myself useful there too. I learned to lay the table, and serve the meals, to sweep the house and run errands. But my father was still firm on one point. I was never allowed to eat in another house. I had to report back to him at every meal-time and at bed-time. He gave me no opportunity to stray from the narrow path he had laid down for me.

CHAPTER EIGHT

My Bad Year

I do not look back with any pleasure on the year when I was nine. I suppose that it must have held many pleasant days, but the incidents that remain vividly in my mind are all dark ones.

I became very sick. I do not know what the sickness was. Neither my parents nor I were interested in its name. We were certain of its cause. Some witch or wizard was trying to steal my life from me. There was a European doctor in Ho, but nobody thought of consulting him. Native doctors from several near-by places were called in, and they consulted together. I remember very little about the first week or two. It is just a confused memory of weakness and pain. I remember being made to drink an infusion of bitter herbs, and to swallow a black powder. I remember the long, dark nights when I could not sleep. Then I remember dimly a period when I had no pain, indeed I seem to have had no feeling at all, but lay in a trance-like state, vaguely aware that my parents were no longer trying to persuade the spirits to return my life to me, but only to give me a peaceful death.

Suddenly, however, when all hope had been lost, I began to recover. One of the first things I became aware of, was the unpleasant feel and smell of my own body. For weeks I had not been bathed, but had been rubbed all over with a mixture of palm-oil and certain herbs. My parents now asked whether it was safe to bathe me. The doctors agreed to this, but stipulated that they should prepare the bath-water. They gathered more herbs and left them in the sun to dry. Then they ground them into a powder, and boiled them in a bucket full of water on the fire. My bath-water was nearly black in colour and had a strong bitter scent.

Towards evening the water was lukewarm, and my mother lifted me out of bed. I was so thin and light that she was able to carry me easily. Steadying me with one hand, she took my nightgown off me with the other. At this point I suddenly took fright at the thought of being bathed in the black water. I made a feeble attempt to run away, and fell down the concrete steps outside the door, on to the stony ground beneath. My father heard the noise of my fall, and my mother's loud cry, and came rushing out of his bedroom.

'You are very stupid!' he shouted at my mother.

'You are not to say that to me,' my mother retorted.

'And why not?' shouted my father. 'Look at that poor child on the ground. This is the boy who cost us so much money and so many sleepless nights. And now that he begins to get well you let him fall. Can't you be more careful with him?'

My overwrought mother began to cry.

'Do you think I did it purposely?' she sobbed.

72

'Well, pick him up then, before I slap you,' my father commanded sternly.

My mother picked me up and began to bathe me, and as she washed me she wept. She wept for many reasons; for the weakness of her child, a living skeleton, with a big head and sunken eyes; for the harshness of her husband, and for her own weariness. She talked as she bathed me.

'You should know you are weak,' she said. 'Why did you run away? God punished you by allowing you to fall down, and then that foolish man came to abuse me. Why do you give me so much trouble?'

I began to shiver, so she hurriedly dried me, smeared my body again with oil, and put me back to bed.

After that I got stronger every day until the doctors pronounced me out of danger. Then they met together to perform a final ceremony, after which I would be allowed to resume my normal life. I looked forward longingly to seeing my friends again, going to the Mission house, eating mangoes, and even going to school.

My parents were required to provide one goat, one sheep, two cockerels, and five pounds. The cockerels had to be black and white, because both black and white wizards might be causing my sickness, and must be placated. The ceremony started at dawn one Sunday morning. The doctors slaughtered the animals and themselves cooked a large meal. A preparation of corn was cooked with the meat, and all our household and friends joined in the festive meal. After this a rare and secret herb was mixed with water and sprinkled on me, and all round the house. The remaining mixture was put in a calabash in our bedroom and I was to drink from it

73

for the next seven days. This was a purification ceremony, designed to drive out any evil spirits that lurked
in the corner of our home. Had it not been performed
the spirits might have returned to trouble me again. Or
they might have attacked some other child in the house
and caused his death. So the whole house was purified,
the doctors departed with their fee and the grateful
thanks of my parents, and I was ready to resume my
normal life.

My father, however, had one more act of thanks-
giving to make. He ordered a 'Missa Cantata' of thanks-
giving to be sung in the parish church, and, after it,
all our friends were invited to our house for refreshments.
My sickness certainly cost my parents a great deal of
money, but they gave it no thought. They were overjoyed at my unexpected recovery.

I stayed in the house for another week and then I
went back to school. At first I found I was too weak to
join wholeheartedly in my friends' activities, but day
by day my strength returned and soon I was my old self.

But it became apparent that the special position I had
held in our household because of my sickness had gone
to my head! As I grew stronger so I became more and
more troublesome. I was filled with a sense of my own
importance. At home I expected to come first in everything, as I had when I was sick. At school I bullied my
friends and disturbed my class.

My father took note of all this. Nothing escaped his
watchful eye. He came to the conclusion that I must be
made to toe the line as soon as possible. Ah well, he soon
got his chance.

Exam. time came, once more I passed and was
promoted. But this time I was promoted into my father's

own class, Standard 1 – for headmasters are also class-teachers. Even now there are not enough teachers to release the headmaster for administrative and supervisory work alone.

On the first morning of the new year I went proudly into the junior school. My classmates were all gathered in the classroom but there was no teacher there. The class-teacher, my father, was busy with his duties as headmaster, and we were directed to wait quietly for him in our classroom. But during the holidays the school had been repainted, and the paint was still slightly wet. All schools were the same – a swish building with the walls whitewashed at the top and painted with coaltar at the bottom. It was the coaltar that was still wet!

We began to play about. Our teacher did not come and we became more and more unruly. One of the boys pressed his hand on to the wet coaltar, and then took hold of my clean white shirt. He left a great black stain. I was so angry that I too pressed my hand on the paint, and then slapped the boy full in the face. The uproar from the classroom brought my father quickly upon the scene. There was immediate silence.

'What is the matter here?' he asked. The other boy at once showed his painty face and told my father the story. But he said it was an accident that he had put the paint on my shirt. On hearing him say this I stepped forward, and began to give my version of the story. No sooner had I begun to speak, however, than my father struck me so roughly that I fell to the ground, and for a minute was stunned. As I sat the rest of the morning in my desk, shaken and silent, I reflected that if this was the way my father welcomed me into his class I could expect a hard year.

At lunch-time I hurried home and reported the whole incident to my mother. I begged her to send me away to attend Standard 1 in some other school. I told her I could not face a year with my father as my teacher.

When my father came in, my mother immediately brought up the subject. She said that he had treated me most unfairly, and that, even had I deserved some punishment, he should have remembered my recent sickness and been more lenient with me.

But my father, as usual, had his reasons. Looking back now I realize that, although the punishments my father dealt out to me were always severe, sometimes brutal, yet they were rarely unjust or unreasonable. Now he explained to my mother, 'Look Edzi, you know the rules in this town. If anyone strikes his neighbour in the face, he must be summoned before the chief. The fine is often heavy – £5, a ram, bottles of gin. If I had taken no notice of this affair and the boy had appealed to his parents, they would have taken the matter up. We are strangers in this town and, in my position, we want to avoid any quarrel with our neighbours. Now, if the child's parents come to see me, I can tell them that I have already dealt severely with Kofi, and they will be satisfied.'

My mother was also satisfied and the matter was left there. But I decided to be very careful and never to report anything to my father, even when I was right. If I was in any difficulty, I went to one of the other two teachers in the junior department, both of whom dealt with me gently.

The work in that class went on well. My father's teaching methods certainly made his children's studies progress. But I was not happy. My father stopped punishing me in the house, and instead reported any bad thing I did to my classmates, and punished me before them all. I suppose in this way he killed three birds with one stone. He avoided distressing my mother so much, he provided an awful warning for the other children, and he increased my shame and humiliation.

The height of it all was the day when I was beaten so much that I could not stand up. That day he really beat me like a snake.

It began as an ordinary schoolday. I went home at lunch-time expecting to get my favourite lunch of rice and stew. I knew that my mother had cooked it for the school-children to buy, and that there had been some left over. But I found that she had cooked another dish for her household's lunch, because she was expecting a lot more customers for the rice and stew. Indeed, there were already several of them buying it as I went in. When they had gone, I asked her for some, but she refused, and told me to go to the kitchen. But I complained, and begged, and in the end got very angry. I went outside and got a big sharp stone. I meant to throw it and break the rice pot. But my aim was not quite as good as I had imagined. I threw it with all my force, missed the rice pot, and hit and cut my mother's leg. My mother screamed, and I was appalled at what I had done, and ran away.

My mother sent for my father, who had not yet returned from school. He came quickly, and she told him what had happened. My father called me. I heard him but did not go. I stood on the dwarf wall of the kindergarten classroom, a short distance away, and yet with a good view of the house. After a few minutes I saw a group of older schoolboys assemble outside the house – evidently they had been sent for. My father came out, spoke a few words to them and pointed at me. The schoolboys spread out and began to walk towards me. Obviously they had been told to surround and capture me. I jumped off the wall and filled my pockets with stones. I realized I had very little chance, for the older children could run faster than me, but I was determined to put up a good fight. I began to shower my pursuers with stones. Some found their mark, and the children who were hit dropped out of the chase, but the noise had attracted others and some were coming at my back. My stones gave out and I had no time to collect more. I took to my heels and ran, and, like a thief, I was chased and caught.

Tired and afraid I was taken to my father. He quietly dismissed the children and took me to his bedroom and locked me in. There I was left while he had his lunch. I think that perhaps that half-hour was my nearest taste of hell. I was terrified of the unknown punishment that I would receive, and I was filled with remorse for the way I had hurt my mother and some of my friends, and I was tired and hungry.

My father finished his lunch, opened the door and quietly told me to go and stand beside his table. He came and looked at me. 'What did you do?' he asked. At once I burst into tears. 'You are a very wicked boy,' he told me. 'For some time now you have been behaving badly, and treating your mother without proper respect. Now look how you have hurt her. This is a very serious thing you have done, and I shall have to make you understand how serious.' He stood up and fetched a rope of coconut fibre. 'Bring out your hands,' he said. Helplessly I did so, and my wrists were tied together.

For a moment he stood and looked at me gravely again. Then he led me to his bedroom door, lifted me up, and so secured the rope that I was left hanging by my hands. Then he took a loose end of the rope and whipped me. I cried out for help and my mother came weeping and begged that I should be pardoned.

'If you come nearer with that nonsense,' was my father's answer, 'I shall whip you too.'

As if he could no longer bear what he was doing, he suddenly stopped, and left me hanging by my hands. The pain in my wrists and shoulders grew unbearable, and somehow I managed to climb up and sit on the top of the door. My father came again and whipped my bare legs with the rope. This time I screamed so loudly that a neighbour knocked at the door and asked what was happening. My father brought me down from the door and untied my hands. He hurriedly got ready to go to school, but before he left he warned me, 'If you dare come late to school you will be in more trouble, and that will be a school case, where no one can come in and save you.'

I ran to school with tears running down my cheeks, and with aching wrists, and bruises all over my body. I managed to be in my place in time. My father entered, sat down and marked the register without calling the names. He just looked at his class to see who was present and who was absent, and marked the register in silence. There was an unnatural stillness about the classroom. One look at my face and one at my father's had told my classmates that there was trouble.

When he had finished his marking my father told the class to repeat together the Fourth Commandment. Their childish voices rang out, 'Honour thy father and mother,

79

that thy days may be long in the land which the Lord thy God hath given thee.' '*Who* has broken this Commandment of God today?' my father asked. There was no reply. Then he requested that each child should stand and say whether he had broken this Commandment this day. One after another, they stood and said, 'No'. I sat in the end desk in front, and he started with the boy in the front desk far right, so that it came to me the last.

When my turn came I could not answer. I could only cry again. My father pointed at me. 'Look at the sinner,' he commanded the class. 'This is the one who has disobeyed God's Commandment.' He made the class repeat the Commandment again. The other children were all seated, but I was made to stand up where all could see me.

My father then sent the class prefect to cut six canes from the flexible nim-trees outside. There was no more doubt now as to what was before me. I was stretched on the front desk, my arms and legs tightly held by eight of the boys, two to each limb. My father gave me twenty-five strokes on my buttock bringing each stroke down with all his force. The deathly stillness of the room was broken only by my screams, the whistle of the cane as it came down, and a terrified sob or two from some of the other children. As he brought the cane down for the last time my father said, 'And one for the Kaiser.' Was it our German rulers who taught our people such cruelty?

My captors were told to release me, and my father ordered me to stand up. I could not do so. He repeated his order, and I struggled from the desk and fell to the floor. At once his heavy shoe went into my side. I screamed, and the teacher from Class 3 came in, and

80

picked me up, and carried me home to my mother.

When my mother saw me she was filled with so much pity that she held me in her arms like a baby, and wept. She immediately ordered that water should be put on the stove to heat, and she prepared that rice and stew which I had so much wanted an hour before. But now I had no appetite. I could not eat it. I was in great pain. My mother gently bathed my whole body with warm water, and laid warm cloths across my swollen buttocks. Then she wrapped me in a blanket and put me into her own bed.

I was not able to get up from my bed for a whole week, and my mother and father did not speak a word to each other. My mother wept quietly as she went about her work. My father sat silent and grim in his sitting-room.

That experience, so dearly bought, shaped my whole future. From that day I knew that I, and only I, would bear the consequences of whatever I did. That day saw the end of my childhood. From then on I knew that I must stand on my own feet.

But even the darkest days pass, and pain of body and spirit subsides with time. The end of the year came at last, and I was promoted to another class, to be taught by a teacher who, to me, was always gentle and loving.

CHAPTER NINE

New Interests

The English say that the darkest hour comes before the dawn, and certainly that was true of my school life. The year I spent in Standard 2 was as unlike that of Standard 1 as it is possible to be. My new teacher was an easy-going man with a real affection for children. He seemed to like us as we were, not only for what he could make of us. He was especially gentle with me. The other children, so used to my father's rule, took advantage of his leniency and the standard of work went down. It did not, however, have that effect on me. At first I kept up my standard of neatness, accuracy, and attention, because my father kept a watchful eye on my progress and behaviour, although I was no longer in his class, and he inspected my exercise books regularly. But soon I was doing my best simply to please my teacher, and to earn his praise. In a few weeks I soared up to the top of the class and began to enjoy school.

I remember vividly the first day I was called out to the front of the class, not to be punished, but to be praised. The teacher entered the room, picked out an exercise book from the pile on his table, and said, 'Kofi, come here.' The room swam before my eyes, I felt sick, I could not move. How often during the year before, had I heard those words. They were always the prelude to misery. I felt again in imagination the stare of forty pairs of self-righteous eyes; heard again the cold cutting voice of my father reciting my disobedience or stupidity to forty pairs of ears; felt again the cut of the cane, and heard my own voice sob and gasp, although I had vowed to myself that this time I would make no sound.

But I was bewildered. I had nothing on my conscience. The exercise book which my teacher held contained nothing but my most painstaking work. I forced myself to my feet. Well, this teacher's worse punishments were light to anyone who had been in Standard 1. But my heart cried out, 'Not from you, not from you.'

Out in the front of the class I raised my eyes slowly to my teacher's face. He was smiling. He put a hand on my shoulder and turned me to face the class. 'Look,' he said, 'Kofi is the youngest of you all, and he has done a beautiful piece of work. Can you all see?' he asked, holding my opened exercise book towards them. 'Not a single mistake, beautiful figures, straight lines drawn with a ruler, proper spacing. Very good indeed, Kofi. Children, give him a clap.'

The class burst into applause. The same children who had so often watched my humiliation. Here, in the place that had held so much terror for me, I was actually being praised. The delightful experience was too wonderful for me to bear. I burst into tears, grabbed my exercise book from my astonished teacher, and ran back to my desk, amid the amazed exclamations and laughter of my friends.

But my teacher was a wise man. He made no comment, but refrained from praising me in front of the class for the next few weeks. Instead he gave me a quiet 'Well done,' as he passed me in my desk. Later he called me out to work sums on the blackboard, or to point out places on a map, until I forgot that the front of the class was ever an undesirable place to be.

Many new doors opened for me that year. My teacher was a keen Scouter and he started a Wolf Cub pack. I was one of the first to be enrolled and soon became a Sixer. Cubbing was a great adventure for me and gave me many memorable hours. Through it I developed a keen interest in nature study, and spent many a Saturday morning watching birds, snakes and animals. My Cubmaster was in charge of Scouting in the area and he took me with him on the back of his motor-bike when he visited other packs. These days were full of joy for me. I was out for whole days at a time with someone who loved me and was really interested in me. There was the tremendous excitement and exhilaration of the ride on the motor-bike. At the end of it there were Cub meetings and games at which I could not only enjoy myself freely but also show off as a Cub of some experience and the Scoutmaster's assistant! And there was no worry, as there so often was, spoiling my happiest times, of disapproval when I returned home. My father trusted and approved of this teacher and was pleased to let me be with him. In fact between this teacher and my father, the one so gentle and the other so stern, there grew a friendship which I found impossible to understand. My teacher shielded me from my father, but would hear no word against him. His methods in the classroom were the opposite of my father's, and yet there appeared to be no conflict between them as to the proper running of the school. Looking back now I wonder whether my teacher saw in my father a man that no one else suspected. A man, unsure of himself, afraid to show affection in case it should be mistaken for weakness. A man who had a real concern for the welfare and character of his pupils and his children, but who knew no other way of keeping them on the straight and narrow path, than by a sternness that was never relaxed. A man who could have loved and been loved if only he had trusted love. In those days I believed that my father had been born without a heart. When I read of the angel with the flaming sword which guarded the gate of paradise, I saw him in my mind in the likeness of my father with his cane. But, somehow, because of my father's friendship with my teacher, I slipped past him into paradise.

There was an Empire Day when I led the whole parade. This holiday was made much of when I was a boy. For days beforehand school rules were relaxed and lessons forgotten. We built shelters of palm branches round the school playing-field to shield our guests from the burning sun. We swept and weeded and decorated the compound, we tidied and cleaned the school. We rehearsed our songs and plays and recitations. And we practised for the sporting events. These included things like three-legged races, sack races and obstacle races that caused the onlookers much amusement and the runners much embarrassment. What set the days of preparation apart for me, and made them seem like holidays, was that we wore any old clothes to school, so that our uniforms could be washed and starched and pressed. (Few children then had more than one school uniform.)

On the great day we arrived at school by six o'clock, our uniforms stiff with starch, the brown skin of our legs and arms and faces gleaming with cleanliness and oil, our curly black hair fiercely brushed and parted. Accompanied by the school-band, and joined by clubs and organizations, we marched singing through the town. Then we assembled on the school-field where most of the townsfolk, dressed in their brightest clothes, already awaited us. As soon as we were in order the District Commisssioner would arrive. He was a man who inspired us children with great awe. He wore a white uniform and a hat with feathers. He was the man the King had sent and he had only one arm. It was said that he carried a pistol about with him and shot dead anyone who made a remark about his missing arm. They told us that on one occasion a three-year-old child on his mother's back had pointed at the District Commissioner, and called out a rude remark. The District Commissioner had torn him from his mother's back, whirled him round his head, and hurled him into the river. I do not know if this was true, but we believed it, and the mere mention of the District Commissioner's name was enough to make a naughty child behave. I remember that one day I came suddenly face to face with him, and was so terrified that I ran straight home and hid under my mother's bed, and did not come out till the evening.

But on Empire Day the District Commissioner could be stared at with impunity. The Cubs and Scouts met him at the entrance to the school-field, and escorted him to his place on the dais. Then the sports and games,

86

the speeches and songs followed each other through the long hot morning, until even the children were tired and thirsty. But the whole gathering brightened when the time came for the highlight of the day, the March Past. School after school, clubs and organizations in their uniforms, flags flying, bands playing, marched round the field, halted in front of the dais, saluted the flag and marched on. And the whole procession was led by the Cubs with myself at the head. It was my moment of glory. I wore my cap on the side of my head and affected a slight limp – not enough however to make the rhythm of my steps defective! As I turned to salute I found myself looking full into the face of my father, and he smiled at me.

Then there was the week I went to camp. At first I was refused permission to go. My father did not approve of any of us being away from home even for a week. But I wept and refused to eat till both my mother and my Cubmaster came to plead for me. And then, the night before we were to go, my mother had another baby, my little brother Kobla. How I wished I had not begged to go to camp! I wanted to stay and hold the baby and take part in the family rejoicing. I enjoyed the camp but I remember most clearly the joy of taking my baby brother in my arms when I returned, and the big meal my mother cooked for me.

Yes, there were many pleasant days in my life that year and many interesting occupations. And it was in that year, when I suppose I was about eleven years old, that I first fell in love.

Her name was Tona. She was in the junior school, and so finished her lessons for the day twenty minutes before I did. However, she hung about and waited till

I came out of the classroom, and we snatched a few minutes' conversation. I do not know what we talked about. I know that on the days when I did not see her I was restless and miserable. Saturdays and Sundays I spent more time with her but at the cost of much deceit and risk. Every Saturday I asked permission to go to the Mission for confession, and every Sunday evening I said I was going to benediction. What my parents thought of this sudden increase in piety I do not know. Some good spirit must have been on my side for they never refused permission and never discovered that I did not actually go to confession or attend benediction. Instead I sat in the fork of a tree near the chapel, hidden by the leaves, and Tona swung on the bough below and we talked. She always smelt clean and fragrant. And she was good and gentle and innocent.

Nevertheless, she knew something of women's wiles and sometimes made me jealous by being friendly with other boys. It was after one of these estrangements that I received the first letter I had ever had in my life. It said 'You are the only one I think of,' and it was from Tona. At the end of that year Tona and I both carried off the first prize for our school work – she in her class and I in mine. We were praised and congratulated by our families and friends, but the only praises we cared for were each other's.

We met in our tree and promised each other that we would study harder than ever. We would win scholarships, go to college, travel overseas, come back rich, do great things and have wonderful times. We would help each other. There was nothing that we could not do together.

But we had reckoned without the witch.

CHAPTER TEN

The Witch

At the beginning of the month, after my mother had been
to the town to buy her stock, the house was full of sacks
and crates. There were sacks of rice, sacks of sugar and
sacks of flour. There were crates of sardines and pil-
chards, of corned beef and yellow soap. There were rolls
of bright cotton cloth, tins of cooking oil and drums of
kerosene. The store and my mother's bedroom were
crowded with boxes, and the room where I slept with
the older boys housed the overflow of my mother's wares.

One night I found that there was not room for all of us
to put down our mats and I was soon crowded out by the
bigger ones. I wandered round looking for a place to
sleep. My father was working at his books in his sitting-
room, my mother and her girls were cooking in the
kitchen, the little ones were asleep and the bigger boys
playing cards in their room. I felt very alone, and I began
to like the feeling. I stood on the veranda and watched
the clouds moving across the face of the moon so that
the night grew brighter and darker. A night-bird flew

past me and rested in a tall tree. I found myself saying, 'Alone, up high, like a bird.' The words, and the idea, sounded wonderful to me and I repeated them again and again.

In my mother's room was a pile of sacks of rice, rising almost to the ceiling. I climbed to the top of it and found that there was just room for me to sit without bumping my head. I lay down and felt wonderful, alone, up high like a bird. But I could not sleep and gradually I began to be afraid. The shadows moved and took on strange shapes. The leaves of a tree, moved by the breeze, slid round the edge of the window frame, like boneless fingers. I wished my mother would come to bed. I wished that I had made a fuss and brought my father out of his sitting-room to insist that I was given room in the bedroom with the boys. I tried repeating my words to myself but they had lost their magic. However, eventually, I must have fallen into an uneasy sleep, although it seemed to me that I still lay awake on my high bed watching the shadows.

I looked towards the door and saw it opening slowly. I was gripped by terror. I tried to scream but no sound came. I tried to move but my limbs were dead. A man came into the room, closed the door silently and turned towards me. He had no face. With a tremendous effort I screamed, and woke up to hear a small harsh sound coming from my throat. There was no man there. I stumbled and slid down from the pile of sacks, whimpering with fear, and hurled myself across the room and out on to the veranda.

My father's lamp still burned in the sitting-room, my mother and the girls still worked and chattered in the kitchen. I had only slept for a few minutes. All my wish to be alone had vanished. I wanted nothing but human company. I began to cross the compound to go to the kitchen but before I reached there I heard my mother call out, 'Look, a witch!'

I ran the last few yards out of the night into the warm friendly kitchen, and joined my mother and her girls at the window. They were watching a small dark bird that flew across the moonlit sky. As we watched, the bird glowed with an unearthly light. Another few seconds and the light faded. Then it came again and, alternately in light and darkness, the witch-bird flew towards the house.

For a moment there was silence and then the shouting began. Other people had seen the witch-bird and men and boys were out hunting it. Stones and sticks were hurled at it but the bird flew steadily on. It turned, glowing, and my mother whispered with relief, 'It is not coming here.' Then a hunter arrived with a gun and was greeted with cheers. He aimed and fired, but the bird flew higher and faster and disappeared towards the other end of the town.

'Where is it going?' I asked my mother. 'What will it do?'

'It will suck the blood of some poor soul,' she said. 'It is the spirit of a witch. While her body lies asleep on her bed her spirit in the form of a bird goes out to kill her enemy.'

'Who is it, mother?' I asked.

'Who knows?' she answered. 'If the hunter had killed it the witch would have been found dead on her bed, a body without a soul. But it was protected by witchcraft. You saw how the hunter's bullet did it no harm.'

She turned back to her cooking. I stayed with her till

she went to her room, and I spent the rest of the night under her bed.

The next day Tona was not in school. I sent a friend of mine to find out why. They said she was sick. The day after that she was dead.

My father announced her death at the morning assembly. He did not know that she had been anything more to me than another child in the school. I felt nothing but shocked disbelief at first, but during the arithmetic lesson my tears began to flow and to drop on my book.

My teacher asked what was the matter, and I told him I had a bad headache, and he sent me home. My mother was not in the house. She had gone to sympathize with Tona's mother and I followed her to Tona's house.

From some distance away I could hear the women wailing. The compound was crowded with people and I slipped unnoticed amongst them. Neighbours always gather to show their sympathy with the family of one who dies, but it seemed to me that this gathering was larger than usual and more excited. There were grave discussions taking place among the old men, as well as the customary exchange of greetings, and the offering and accepting of palm wine. There were women talking in angry tones as well as those who were weeping. I pushed my way to the centre of the crowd where Tona lay on her mat. They had dressed her in a more beautiful cloth than she had ever worn when she was alive. There were gold chains round her neck and flowers wilting on her pillow. She did not look like Tona. She had gone already. I stood looking at her and did not know what to do. My mother saw me and led me to greet the head of the family, Tona's grandfather.

The old man looked at me thoughtfully. 'Kofi,' he said. 'He also shines at school.' He turned his gaze to my mother. 'Be careful,' he warned her. 'Do not arouse the enmity of those who are jealous.' My mother nodded her head and we left the compound.

'What did he mean?' I asked her, but she shook her head, and asked me instead why I was not at school. I told her I had a headache. Her eyes filled with fear and she felt my skin and hurried me home.

'What made Tona die?' I asked her, but she would not answer me. 'Do not speak of it,' she said.

Tona was buried that afternoon and almost the whole town followed her to her grave. I stood outside our house knowing that the coffin must pass me on its way to the cemetery. I heard the procession approaching but the sounds that accompanied it frightened me. Instead of the usual singing there was an angry roar. The people were shouting and wailing. My mother and father came out and stood with me as the procession came in sight. Four men carried the coffin but they were behaving in an alarming manner. They crossed and recrossed the road, sometimes running forward, sometimes backward, sometimes standing quite still for a minute or two, so that the procession made very little progress. A crowd of people danced and shouted around it. In the midst of them was a young white priest, obviously afraid. Tona was a baptized child and he had intended to follow the coffin to the cemetery and say some prayers at the grave. When he saw my father he left the crowd and joined us outside the house.

'Headmaster,' he said, 'what is it? Are these men drunk?'

93

'No, Father,' my father answered. 'They are bewitched.'

The coffin reached us. The four men appeared to be in a trance. Their eyes stared without blinking, their movements were jerky. But they acted exactly in unison. Although the movements of the coffin were so irregular, the men acted in perfect accord with it.

'What does it mean?' the priest asked again. 'The child will not go to the cemetery,' my father told him. 'She did not die a natural death. She wishes to be avenged.' Just then the coffin turned abruptly and the bearers set off at a run down a side road opposite our house. With a roar the crowd followed it. There was no hesitating now. Coffin and crowd continued straight down the hot road till they were lost to our sight in the dust they made. My mother started to follow them but my father called her back. 'Do not get involved in this,' he ordered her.

He turned to the young priest. 'Go home, Father,' he said. 'There is nothing you can do.' 'Where will they bury her?' the priest asked. 'They will bring her back to the cemetery in the end,' my father told him. 'But now she goes to show them the witch.'

I began to understand. The witch-bird had flown over the town. Tona had died. Her body refused to rest until she had shown us her murderer. A great horror came over me. Someone lived who hated Tona enough to kill her. But who would hate Tona? Who could kill Tona? My fear turned to fury. The witch who killed Tona should herself be killed. I knew now why the women talked in angry voices, why the men danced and shouted. I was one of them. My heart was filled with vengeance.

My parents went back into the house. Although

firmly believing that Tona had been killed by witch-craft they did not wish to take any part in seeking out her murderer. My father's position as headmaster of a Mission school made it necessary to separate himself from his people on such occasions. I remained outside the house waiting to know what had happened. When the sun was setting the procession returned. The coffin was quiet now. The bearers had been replaced by four different young men. The first four lay in an exhausted sleep by the roadside where they had fallen when the magic left the coffin. The people were singing and the procession made its way to the cemetery.

I followed and saw Tona laid to rest in the earth. Her grandfather swore on her grave that her death should be avenged.

On the way home a schoolfriend told me that the coffin had forced the carriers to run straight into the compound of a house at the other end of the town. Everyone was satisfied that the witch lived there, but as there were several people in that house the god of the town would be asked to show which one was guilty.

It was several days later that the gong-gong was beaten in the late afternoon and the whole town called to assemble outside the chief's house. The crowd was large when I got there and I could see nothing, but I climbed up a very high tree and, seated in the swaying branches, I watched the whole scene.

After all were assembled the door opened and the chief emerged. He was a middle-aged man dressed in a glow-ing kente cloth, wearing a gold crown on his head and sandals on his feet. He was preceded by his horn-blower and accompanied by his linguist, bearing his staff of office, and the elders of the town. A small boy of my own age carried the royal stool, and another walked in front of the chief, acknowledging on his behalf the greetings of the crowd. The chief himself did not change expression from one of stern gravity. The stool was set down outside the house and the chief and his party sat.

Then came the fetish priest, a tall old man, naked to the waist, and his assistants. Some of these, too, were children no older than myself – little girls in white skirts, their arms and the upper parts of their bodies smeared with white clay, and covered with strings of white cowrie-shells.

The priest stationed himself by an altar that had been set up in the compound, and poured a libation to the god asking that the truth might be revealed.

Another group then came from the chief's house and in the centre of it were three women. Their clothes were torn and they stumbled and wept. Obviously they had been roughly treated. Two were old and ugly. The other was about my mother's age and plump and comely. They were the occupants of the house that Tona's coffin had entered, and they all denied that they had killed the girl. The crowd began to jeer at them and threaten them. A few stones were thrown. But the chief ordered the people to be still.

Three cocks were brought and given to the priest's assistants. The first old woman was brought before the altar and warned to speak the truth or the god would surely kill her. She threw herself on her knees and swore that she was not a witch. The priest took the first cock and with a sharp knife cut its throat half-way across. Then he threw it on the ground. Amid a breathless silence the cock struggled to its feet, ran a few steps and collapsed and died on its back, it breast uppermost. The

96

crowd roared. The god had accepted the woman's answer. She had spoken the truth. She was innocent and free. She fell sobbing on the ground, till her friends came and helped her to her feet.

The second old woman was brought forward. She too denied that she was a witch and the same ritual was followed. Her cock too died on its back and the god acknowledged her innocence.

Now they brought the third woman before the altar. The crowd grew restless and an angry muttering prevented me from hearing what the woman answered. But she stood upright and looked proud and defiant. The priest took the cock in his hand, but then he paused and in a loud and stern voice which silenced the crowd he cried, 'Take care, woman, what you do. If you are guilty the god will surely reveal it. And if you have not spoken the truth the god will surely kill you.' He took up his knife but before he had time to use it the woman fell to the ground, her limbs twitching and foam coming from her mouth. The crowd roared. The priest put down the knife and let the cock flutter away. Two of his assistants raised the woman to her feet and held her till her strength returned. Then, trembling, she confessed that she was a witch. She was exhorted by the priest and his assistants to confess all her crimes.

Somewhere a drum began to beat, low and insistent. I began to feel faint from the heat and my cramped position. The scene on which I looked seemed to go far away and became small and unreal although I still saw and heard it clearly. I was looking on the witch who had flown over my house and gone on to murder Tona. In a few moments I should hear it from her own lips. More drums began to beat, their different rhythms inter-

97

weaving. The woman said that she had exchanged the life of her own child long ago for her witchcraft power, and had had no more children. Tona's mother had taunted her and jeered at her, speaking of Tona's health and beauty and her success at school, and reviling her for her childless state. Witnesses were called to confirm that this was true. Tona's mother was called and sternly rebuked.

Then again the woman was urged to confess that she had murdered Tona by witchcraft and she said, 'It is true.'

Then the drums began to beat more loudly and the people jeered and shouted abuse at the woman. She was stripped naked and then covered roughly with a torn mat. A few broken pots and old pieces of cloth and a bottle of water were tied in a bundle and put on her head. With shouts and songs and blows she was driven to the edge of the town. I went too. I wanted to see her killed. I was filled with hatred and the desire to see her die.

But when the crowd halted at the end of the town they did not kill her. They told her that if ever she entered Ho again she would be beaten to death, and then they drove her into the bush.

Where would she go? Her nakedness would proclaim that she was a fugitive from justice. Anyone who saw her would know she was a witch. No one would give her food or shelter. The snakes and scorpions and driver ants would endanger her life in the bush. The ghosts and spirits would drive her mad with fear. Probably she would not live long. But she had a chance, and Tona had had no chance.

I walked home quickly for it was almost dark and it

was one of my father's strictest rules that we must never be out after dark. This thought brought my mind back to everyday life and turned it from the hatred that was consuming me. Then I thought of Tona's grandfather and how he had cautioned my mother. 'Kofi shines at school. Be careful.' So Tona had died because she came top of her class and her mother had boasted. Suddenly I felt very small and lost. What could I make of a world where to do well at school endangered one's life? My father would not accept anything second-best from me, my mother would boast as Tona's mother had done. And anyway, Tona was gone. All my great plans had been hers too. Now I was alone and afraid, bewildered in a lonely and dangerous world.

I reached home and sat on the ground and wept. But I did not know if I was weeping for myself or for Tona, or even for the lost witch alone in the bush.

CHAPTER ELEVEN

The Children in Trouble

I was very jealous of the little boy, Bolo, from Shiamlolo.
He was nearer to me in age than anyone else in the
house and so we were often together. He was two years
older than I, but his small size and the fact that he had
to learn our language put him on my level. We were
often sent together on errands or given jobs to share.
But it seemed to me that my parents liked him better
than me. My mother entrusted him with her accounts
because he was good at arithmetic, and my father
employed him on copying out notices and records
because he had neat handwriting. This meant he was
more with them than I was and that he more often
earned a word of praise from them. He, on his side,
objected to being classed with me, because he was older
and cleverer than I, and felt that he belonged to the
group of older boys. So we played a perpetual game of
trying to get each other into trouble without getting
into trouble ourselves. And this was not very easy
in a house headed by a father who knew boys

inside out, and took his parental duties very seriously!

One night, some slight noise wakened me, but I did not immediately move or open my eyes. I heard Sika go softly out of the room and thought that he had gone to the latrine. But a few minutes later Bolo, too, tiptoed out. Now I was wide awake. I moved into a comfortable position from which I could see Bolo's mat through half-closed eyes and pretended to be asleep. After ten minutes or so the two returned and softly closed the door.

'Wake George up!' directed Bolo. 'Why not leave him asleep? Then we can share this between us,' suggested Sika. 'You know he'd find out. Last time I tried to double-cross him he nearly twisted my arm off,' said Bolo ruefully.

'What about Kofi?' asked Sika. 'No, not him, he's too much of a baby,' jeered Bolo. 'One word from the Old Man and he'd give the whole show away.'

I almost sat up and indignantly denied being a baby, but my curiosity was greater than my pride. I lay still and listened and watched.

Sika and Bolo brought out of their cloths handfuls of sweets and a packet of biscuits, a tin of salmon and a tin of condensed milk. George was woken, and the three boys had a fine feast. The tin of salmon was opened with George's pocket-knife, and the contents spread on some of the biscuits. When these were eaten, the thick sweet milk was spread on the rest of the biscuits, and the tin cleaned out with the boys' fingers. My mouth watered and I was furiously angry with the boys. Not, I am afraid, because they were stealing my mother's stock, but because they had not included me in their nocturnal adventures.

'Don't forget to alter the book, Bolo,' said George, as they settled down to sleep.

'And don't forget to hide the tins,' retorted Bolo.

So that was how it was done. Bolo falsified my mother's accounts so she never knew her stock was short.

The next day Bolo and I were put on duty at my mother's long table in the lunch-hour. An idea came to me. Making sure that Bolo was watching I slipped a tin of sardines and a flat tin of toffees into the pocket of my shorts.

'Here, what are you doing?' asked Bolo.

'I shall be hungry tonight,' I answered.

'I'll tell your mother,' threatened Bolo.

'Oh, no, you won't,' I said. 'Because I can tell her about the salmon, and biscuits, and sweets, and milk that you and Sika and George steal in the night.' Bolo was silent. I pressed home my advantage. 'And you can alter the numbers in my mother's book, and then I'll share these with you tonight.'

Bolo appeared to be convinced.

'All right,' he said.

That night I was too excited to sleep. As soon as the house was still I woke Bolo. But, to my disappointment, he refused to wake the older boys. 'No,' he said, 'we never go on a raid two nights running. Let's just eat your things. Then you can join us tomorrow.'

We ate the stolen goods, but somehow it wasn't much fun. Sardines are difficult things to eat without a spoon or a piece of bread, and they do not mix well with toffees in the stomach of an excited and anxious small boy at midnight. I was glad when we had finished and Bolo said, 'I'll take the tins out, and hide them, Kofi.' He tiptoed out, and I was asleep before he returned.

The next evening I came in from playing to find a definite atmosphere about the house. My father, wearing his glasses, was studying my mother's book, while she watched him with an annoyed and worried expression. Bolo stood near by, pencil in hand.

'Well, Edzi,' said my father. 'The boy seems to be right. You are a tin of sardines and a tin of toffees short. Oh! well,' he teased her, 'you are a rich woman. You can afford a few unexplained losses.'

But my mother was not satisfied. For once it was she who wanted the truth probed out.

'I know, Master,' she explained. 'But for some time now I have fancied that things were disappearing, though Bolo always reported that the numbers were right. The other day I felt sure I had a full dozen packets of biscuits on the shelf in the store, but there were only eleven. Bolo thought I was mistaken because we had eleven written in the book. But this time Bolo agrees with me. I wonder if one of the house-girls or -boys is a thief?'

The sardines and toffees, which had not troubled me all day, suddenly made me feel sick. My mother, reluctantly, could imagine that one of the boys or girls in her charge was a thief, but how would she feel if she found out her own son was one, too?

What had gone wrong? Had Bolo forgotten to alter the numbers? Then he spoke again and I understood that he had deliberately betrayed me.

'It was at the end of the lunch hour yesterday that I found they were missing,' he said.

'Who was looking after your things then?' my father asked my mother.

'Bolo and Kofi,' she replied.

'Well,' said my father shrewdly, 'Bolo wouldn't be so eager to report it if he had anything to do with it. Kofi, do you know anything about this?'

'No, Papa,' I said.

'Did you sell any sardines,' he asked.

'Yes, Papa, quite a lot.'

'Did you give one too many to anyone, do you think?'

'I don't know, Papa. I don't remember.'

'Did you sell any toffees?'

'No, Papa.'

'There was only one tin on the table,' put in Bolo. 'That is how I missed it.' My father looked at him hard.

'I wonder why you are so sure of this?' he said. George and Sika came in then and he looked at them too. Then he said to my mother, 'I think I'll just look round the boys' room, Edzi.'

I felt much better. There was no evidence in the room. It occurred to me then that I did not know where Bolo had hidden the tins, but I had no doubt that they were well hidden.

Then my father called my name, and his voice made my heart leap with terror.

'Kofi! Come here!' he called. I went into the room. My father stood before my open box, and roughly hidden under the top cloth were the empty sardine and toffee tins.

'So my son is a thief and a liar,' he said. The mixture of emotions that welled up in me seemed to stop me breathing. I was broken-hearted because it was true – I was a thief. But I was also terrified, because I had not forgotten what my father had done to me when I had broken another of the Commandments. And I was furiously angry with Bolo because of his treachery.

My mother had followed me to the doorway, and now she stood looking in horror from my box to me, and then to my father.

'Mama,' I cried. 'Mama, please! It isn't true!'

'What is not true, Kofi?' asked my father. 'Is it not true that you stole your mother's sardines and toffees?'

What could I say? It was true, and yet I was somehow the injured party.

'Yes, it is true,' I said, 'but ...'

'Well,' said my father, 'but ... what?'

Suddenly I wanted the whole thing over whatever it cost me. It was too horrible. I could not bear the long interrogations that would go on if I told about the other boys.

'But, please, Papa, it is the only time I have taken anything. Truly it is. And I'm very, very, sorry.'

'You had better tell your mother you are sorry. They were her things that you stole.' I turned to my mother.

'Mama, I am sorry, I beg your pardon,' I cried.

I was shivering and sweating at the same time. Then, without warning, I was sick. I had only time to rush out of the room into the compound. My distress was so obvious that it softened even my father's heart.

'Go to bed, Kofi,' he said. 'We will speak of this in the morning.'

I cried myself to sleep. The other boys did not come near me. When I next woke it was dark, and they were all asleep on their mats. I cried again and slept till morning.

My father called me to his sitting-room as soon as I was dressed.

The tins were on the table in front of him.

'Kofi, who stole these things from Mama?'

'I did, Papa,' I whispered.

'Did anyone tell you to do it?'

'No, Papa.'

'Has anyone else been stealing mama's things?'

'Please, Papa, I don't know,' I answered.

He was silent for a long minute. Then he began to do some very strange things. He got up, but he did not go to get his cane. He went instead to his desk, and took from it a nail, a hammer, and a piece of string. I was interested, in spite of my distress.

'Kofi, your mother came to me at dawn this morning. You know that it has always been the custom of our people, as far back as anyone can remember, to hold serious and important talks at dawn. It is the time when advice is given and received. The time when wrongs are righted, and forgiveness asked. It is the time when people come to plead for help. Your mother came to plead for you, Kofi.' At this my tears broke out afresh. 'She believes you when you say you have never stolen anything else. She begs me not to beat you. I have promised her not to, this time.'

I was still.

'But,' he went on, 'you must be punished. I am going to tie these tins round your neck, and you will wear them the whole day.'

I watched him, fascinated, as he banged a hole in the sardine tin, and in the toffee tin, and in the lid, and threaded them on the string. Then he tied them round my neck.

The few steps that it took me to get out of my father's sitting-room were the hardest I ever took. I tried to hide the tins under my shirt, but the bulges were obvious and the jagged sardine tin cut my skin. I asked permission to stay away from school, but was refused. I thought of taking off the tins and running away. But I had nowhere to run to. Anyone to whom I ran would return me to my father. Step by step I got through the day. I do not remember a great deal about it – only a terrible feeling of desolation. My class-teacher told me to stay in the classroom at recreation time, and so I was spared some of my schoolmates' stares and jeers. My father himself sent for me before the end of afternoon school and told me I might go home early to avoid going to assembly.

'Go to your mother,' he told me, 'and tell her that, if she is satisfied that you have learned your lesson, she may take off the tins.' She took them off at once, and there the matter might have ended if she had not asked me one question. 'Kofi,' she said, 'why did you put the tins in your box?' Then all my resolution broke.

'I didn't put them there! Bolo put them there! He got me into trouble purposely! He wanted Papa to beat me. That is why he didn't alter the figures in your book.'

'In my book?' she echoed.

'Yes. When anyone steals anything he alters the figures so you won't know.'

'So I *was* right about the biscuits and other things,' my mother cried. Then she turned on me angrily. 'And you have known all about this and said nothing! That makes you just as bad as those who stole.'

'No, Mama, truly!' I cried. 'I only knew about it the day before I stole the things.'

'Who steals them? Is it Bolo?'

'Yes, and the other boys.'

Now I had betrayed them all. In my imagination I heard Bolo's scornful voice whispering, 'He's too much of a baby. One word from the Old Man and he'll give the whole show away.'

I slunk away and lay on my mat. All day I had kept my courage up with two thoughts. One was how happy I should feel when my punishment was over. The other was how proud I should be when the other boys were forced to realize I was not a baby, and did not give them away. Now I had thrown away both those consolations. For the second night running I cried myself to sleep.

The other three boys had a painful interview with my father that evening in the school office. And when they came out their punishment was not over. They spent the whole of the school holidays, which started the next day, clearing, digging and fencing a large patch of bush, for my father to make a farm. They had no play-time at all.

My mother put a lock on her store-door and kept her own accounts. I do not think anyone in the house ever stole from her again, but I do not think she would have known if we had. Her accounts were in such a muddle!

As for me, I was sent to Coventry by the boys. They did not do anything to me. They simply behaved as though I were not there. The house-girls, too, left me in no doubt as to their opinion of me. Only the little children were friendly, and they were too small to be companions. I took to hanging round the Mission house again, as I had done when we first arrived in Ho. I renewed my friendship with the farm-children, who knew nothing of the difficulties of keeping the school-boys' code of honour.

And then I fell into another trouble which made the boys accept me again.

It began with a bicycle. The Father had an old one which stood most of the day against the wall. The farm-children dared me to ride it. I had never been on a bicycle, but somehow I managed to mount it and wobble a few yards before I fell down with a loud crash. The children all laughed, and the noise brought the young Father running out. He was not at all annoyed and stayed to give me a riding lesson. By the end of the morning I was in love with the bicycle! For the next week or two I spent most of my time riding round the Mission compound. My father and the three boys were clearing their farm, my mother and the girls busy with the house and children, and so I was not missed. When the Father saw the trick-cyclist act that I was practising, and had been called in several times to bathe and bind my grazes, he became a little alarmed. The next Sunday he spoke to my father after Mass. 'Head-master, this boy of yours, Kofi, is very fond of riding my bicycle. Have you any objection?' My father, a keen cyclist himself in his younger days, was not displeased. While he chatted with the priest I rushed and got the bicycle and showed off all my tricks. My father was in a genial mood. He laughed, and agreed that I had acquired a remarkable amount of skill in a fortnight. He accepted the priest's assurances that he hardly ever used the bicycle, that I was very welcome to borrow it whenever I liked, and that I was not in any way making a nuisance of myself. He even remarked to the priest in my hearing, 'If he continues to do well at school, and shows me an improvement in his behaviour at home, I will buy him a bicycle at the end of the year.' Then he called me to him and resumed his usual forbidding manner. 'Kofi, you have my permission to amuse yourself on this bicycle that the Reverend Father has so kindly lent you. But only so long as you stay in the Mission compound. There is plenty of room here. You must never take the bicycle out on the road by yourself. Next year, if you have been good I will buy you one and send for my own. Then we can take a ride together. Meanwhile you are forbidden to take this one on to the road. Is that clear?'

It was clear and very reasonable. The road which ran along the edge of the Mission compound was a main motor-road, getting busier every month. I willingly gave my promise.

The next morning and every morning after that I went to Mass. I had a lot of arrangements to make with God. I wanted Him to make my father keep his word, and I wanted Him to help me to keep out of trouble. I also felt it was an act of courtesy to the young priest to go to Mass. It seemed to me the best way to show my appreciation to him for introducing this new delight.

But, perhaps because I am Friday-born, the unlucky day, even God himself seemed to be unable to keep me out of trouble. The day soon came when the temptation of the smooth straight road, and the urgings of my friends, were too much for me. In a kind of daze I rode off the Mission path and out into the road. Almost at once a lorry came speeding along and I took fright, skidded, and fell off into the ditch. Everyone shouted! The lorry drew up with a screech only a few yards from where I lay. The driver jumped out, cursing me roundly, and only the arrival of the young Father prevented him from hauling me off to the police station. It had not occurred to me that there was a right and a wrong side of the road! In the middle of all this confusion I had only one thought, 'Don't let my father find out,' but I was unlucky once again. Bolo, of all people, came along. My father seeing that he was really tired and that his hands were blistered, had given him a half-holiday from bush-clearing, and sent him home to rest. He looked at me and the bicycle and the lorry; consternation, excitement and triumph showed plainly in his face; and he turned and shot off again, back to the farm.

The crowd had largely dispersed when my father arrived. Only myself and the priest and a crowd of children were left, trying to straighten out the bent bicycle. My father's footsteps managed to be heavy even though he wore sandals, and his appearance struck us all with awe even though he wore old clothes for farming. He wasted no words. 'Go into the house, Kofi. You, too, Bolo.' As we went, we heard him begin to apologize for my wickedness to the priest, and to offer to pay for the repair of the bicycle. I turned on Bolo, calling him all the bad words I knew, and vowing that I would repay him before the day was out.

The interview with my father was not pleasant, but might have been worse. The main part of my punishment was that, because I had been so disobedient, he would not consider buying me a bicycle – ever. And that I was never to ride the Father's bicycle – or indeed any bicycle – again. I also got six strokes of the cane on my hand, but this was an ordinary school punishment, often received and taken quite lightly.

I at once set about organizing the next round of the continual match between Bolo and me. But this time I went a long way too far.

There was, somewhere about the house, a long iron

rod. I had picked it up from the builder's oddments that lay about the compound while the new school-block was being built. Now I got it, and stuck one end of it in the kitchen stove. My mother and her girls were in the store, the children were out to play. Leaving the iron in the fire I went outside to where Bolo was idly kicking a ball about, and stood watching him. He threw me one or two anxious glances. I knew he was wondering what had taken place between me and my father. We tried all the time to get each other into trouble, but we often became frightened in case the trouble might be too big. I tried to meet his glances in a friendly and reassuring way. Without saying anything, he kicked the ball in my direction, and I knocked it back, vaguely in his. After two or three of these exchanges I called out, 'Wait a minute!' and ran into the house. I took an old rag and held the end of the iron rod and pulled it out of the fire. The other end was red-hot. I waved it about until the glow died and then ran outside with it. I ran past Bolo with it, shouting, 'Here, catch hold of this!' At once he caught hold of the hot end with both his blistered hands. For a second he seemed too shocked to let go, and then he opened his hands with a terrible cry. Horror-struck, I watched him fall to the ground, his burnt hands held to his body, and the smell of the burnt flesh actually came to my nostrils. I rushed in to my father's sitting-room, where he sat resting for an hour before returning to his farm. 'Papa come! Oh come, quickly!' I wailed. 'What have I done? . . . what have I done?' He ran out with me, and picked Bolo up and carried him into the house. I was shut out of the room while he and my mother dressed Bolo's wounds, and covered him with blankets, and gave him soothing herbal medicines to ease the pain and send him to sleep. Meanwhile, I crouched outside the bedroom door praying that he would not die, and that I might be forgiven.

It was early evening before my weary father and mother asked the inevitable question, 'How did it happen?' I told my story haltingly and in whispers, but truly. They were unable to believe it.

'Did you do this purposely?'

'Yes, Papa.'

'When you put the rod in the fire did you then decide that Bolo should hold the hot end?'

'Yes, Papa, that is why I put it in.'

'But someone else might have touched it.'

'No, Papa, the children were out playing and I watched the door to see that they did not go in.'

'When you took the rod outside what did you do?'

'I called Bolo to hold it. I thought he would think it was a new game.'

'But if you and Bolo are such enemies, as you tell me now, why did you think Bolo would want to play your game?'

'Because I had been playing ball with him just before.'

'Do you mean,' asked my horrified father, 'that you deliberately made friends with him in order to play this horrible trick?'

I could not answer, but I nodded my head.

My father turned away and his despair showed in the droop of his shoulders. He spread out his hands in a gesture of bewilderment.

'This boy,' he said, 'this boy . . . And I have tried so hard.'

'He has told the truth,' said my mother. 'Isn't that

a sign that there is some grace in him? He is young. He did not understand how much pain he was causing.'

'By God,' said my father, suddenly vigorous again, 'he shall understand now!'

He ordered my mother out of the room, and caned my hands again and again, till I also held them sobbing to my body as Bolo had done. But for the first and only time in my young life I bore my father no resentment. I still thought my punishment small in proportion to my crime. When my father ordered me to beg Bolo's pardon, I did not find it too difficult; and when he ordered me to fetch and carry for Bolo, and help him in every way until his hands were healed, I did it willingly.

And it was only a day or two later that I caught a gleam of amusement in Bolo's eyes as I fumbled with the spoon as I tried to feed him with my still sore hands.

'What's the matter?' I asked. 'I bet my hands are better than yours,' he said. 'Let me have a go.'

And when George came in a bit later Bolo and I were feeding each other alternate mouthfuls, giggling and spluttering and generally making a mess all over the place.

'Well, you two seem to be getting on all right,' he said. 'What has all the fuss been about?'

CHAPTER TWELVE

Away from My Parents

When I was twelve I left my father's house and went to live with a master. My father had been transferred again. We were all upset when this news came. We had really put down roots in Ho. My mother was well known and prosperous as a trader. We children had all made good friends and those of us who went to school did well and were happy. And my father was intensely proud of his school. It was his success that led to our move. The Mission authorities decided to transfer him to another struggling young school which he could build up. Our new station was in the south, not too far from our home country, but we found that no comfort. The place was primitive. There were only three classes in the school; the Christians in the community a mere handful. There was no suitable house for us. My parents had to spend their savings in building one, and there was not much opportunity for my mother to re-open her trading. The people here farmed and fished for their food, and there was little money for buying imported luxuries, like tinned food or pretty clothes. It seemed that the family would be poor again. Missionaries in those days did not seem to take such things into account when posting their employees to their different stations. They considered only the use they could make of a teacher, expecting devoted and sacrificial service from him and his family, but giving them no consideration in return.

The worst thing of all to me was that the family would be broken up. Although always in awe of my father, I loved my mother, and adored my little brothers and sisters, and had an easy companionship with the boys in my father's care. Now, all of us who were past the primary school had to leave home. Sika, Bolo and I were put in charge of different masters, and Ami, my sister, had to leave school altogether.

I travelled with my family to their new station and disliked it so much that I was a little consoled about being sent away. There were no latrines in the town. People just went into the bush for this purpose. And water was very scarce. It came from three very deep wells at various points in the village, and was drawn up by a bucket on a rope. This looked easy but was really very difficult. Luckily my father's position entitled him to have water drawn for him, and each morning and evening our tins and buckets would be filled for us.

The time came for the schools to re-open and for me to go to my master. He lived in Keta, the big town of the south, and although it was only ten miles away it was a long and tedious journey. My father sent two young men with me to carry my box and show me the way. We had to walk the five miles to the lagoon, so we started early in the morning. It was a market-day in Keta and the road was crowded with people who were going to buy and sell, so we had plenty of company on the way. The women carried loads of all kinds on their heads; great baskets of produce from their farms, loads of firewood, pitchers of oil. Under their arms some of them carried live fowls, their feet tied together; and many of the women had babies on their backs. There were a lot of young girls too, and a few boys, accompanying their mothers and mistresses, helping to carry their wares. Some of them had small tables and stools upside down on their heads. They would display their goods to the best advantage in the market and sit down comfortably while they did so. Here and there a boy carried a goat or a pig across his shoulders or pulled it along on a string. There was so much to see that I was not bored by my long walk. And because the sun was not yet hot and I had no luggage to carry I was not tired. I began to recover from the sadness which had overcome me when I looked at my sleeping brothers and sisters, and said good-bye to my mother.

It did not seem long before the wide expanse of water, the lagoon, lay before me. Here one of my companions turned back, and the other left me to go and buy food and to arrange for the next part of our journey. I sat on my box and watched the lagoon. The sun was high by now and everything glowed with rich colours. The lagoon water was deep blue and so was the cloudless sky. Lined up before me were the canoes which had not yet been chartered, pulled up on the shore, with the tall coconut palms high above them. Out on the lagoon were other canoes, those that had got an early start. Their single, calico sails were unfurled, and they looked to me like gigantic and beautiful living creatures gliding along. All around me were people bargaining excitedly for places on the canoes for themselves and their loads and their livestock. One by one the canoes were launched into the shallow water. Then the passengers would wade out with their loads on their head and the boatmen would arrange the boxes and baskets so that the weight was properly distributed. The passengers then sat in rows of three on board seats across the canoe. The big canoes carried eighteen passengers.

The two boatmen were very firm about where each passenger should sit. I heard them instructing those on the ends of each row to sit as near the edge as possible. I hoped I would not be given that seat. When everything was arranged to the boatmen's satisfaction they pushed-off, using long bamboo poles forked at the ends. The two of them worked alternately. While one thrust his pole into the water the other withdrew his. When they were far out in the lagoon the sail was set, the poles put down and one boatman steered with a short paddle.

My companion returned, having made an agreement with one of the boatmen, and we hurried to our canoe. It was already out in the water and when I had waded in up to my knees I was still far away from it. My companion was seeing to the safe storing of my box and did not notice my predicament. But a hefty boatman swung me on to his shoulder and deposited me, to my relief, in the centre of one of the seats. We moved off, fast at first, and then the sail was set. There was not a great deal of wind and we did not seem to go very fast. As we got farther away from land on one side of the lagoon and yet seemed to get no nearer to the other, I began to get nervous. I noticed that water was seeping in near my feet. One of the boatmen bailed it out from time to time with a calabash. I became really frightened when I saw him pushing what looked like oily cotton-wool into the crevice where the water entered. I looked round at my companions. Some of the women had babies on their backs and I thought how horrible it would be to see them drown. But no one else appeared to be worried. I saw with astonishment that some of the passengers were actually asleep. I turned round to look at those behind me and a boatman shouted, 'Keep steady, boy!' I felt very foolish and miserable. The voyage seemed endless – it took about two and a half hours – and it was chilly despite the sunshine.

But eventually we neared the shore. The sail and mast were taken down and the canoe punted to the side with the bamboo poles. Everyone scrambled off, stretching their cramped limbs, and taking up their loads again. My box was found and we paid the boatman eightpence for transporting it and us across the lagoon.

Almost at once a man, tall, well-dressed, grave, came to us and addressed me by name.

'You are Kofi?' he said. 'Have you a letter for me?'

My companion gave one, in my father's handwriting, to him.

'Yes, that is right,' said the man. 'I am your master. Come, I will show you the way to the house.'

I followed him, and my companion shouldered the box and followed me.

We were soon at his house, where he introduced me to his mother, and returned to his interrupted work. He was a cashier in a big store. The old lady showed me a shady corner of the veranda. 'You may sit there,' she said, not unkindly. 'I am busy now, but the boy will soon be in.' My companion put down my box and took leave of me. I wanted to send loving messages home to my mother but I did not know what to say. When he left the house I felt terribly alone. Except for the occasional sounds of cooking from the kitchen the house was very quiet. No baby crying, no children playing, no mother scolding or singing. The tears in my eyes began to roll down my cheeks.

Then there was a sudden sound of feet running and a boy a year or two older than me came in. He stopped short at the sight of me and I quickly brushed the tears from my face. The old lady looked out of the kitchen.

'Here is the new boy,' she said. 'Take him and show him round.'

The boy came to me and looked at me. He was handsome and smart and confident. I felt inferior and uncomfortable under his gaze.

Just then our master returned from his work. He walked into his sitting-room and a moment later he called, 'Kosi!'

The boy at once responded, 'Sir!' and was gone in a flash.

'Where is the new boy?' I heard my master ask. 'He is just outside, sir,' answered Kosi. 'Bring him in and come yourself.' Kosi came to fetch me and we went and stood before our master. For a long moment he said nothing but he frowned slightly at me. I felt that I was wrong in some way but I did not know how. Then Kosi gave me a nudge. I looked at him and saw what was wrong. I was standing in a slack way, my hands hanging at my sides, my head down. Kosi stood straight, his feet together, and his hands clasped behind his back. I quickly copied him.

'Yes, that is better,' commented my master. I had learned my first lesson.

'Now Kosi,' he said. 'You will look after Kofi. Show him everything he should know. He will eat and sleep with you.'

'Yes, sir,' responded Kosi. The master turned to me. 'Kofi, do not be afraid. If you are good you will be happy here. I shall look after you just as your father would do. Do you understand?'

'Yes,' I whispered. Again there was a pause and a slight frown. What had I done wrong? Then I remembered. 'Yes, sir,' I corrected myself. 'Very well. Go now, both of you, and see if something is ready for you to eat.' We went, and now my tears flowed freely down my face. Now I was no longer a son in the house. I was a servant.

Although life was pleasant and orderly, and punishments rare and light in that house, yet I found it very difficult to settle down and suffered agonies from homesickness. Now I realized how many compensations there had been for my father's harshness. There was always my mother to run to with my troubles. There were my brothers and sisters to play with. And there was plenty of time to play. Now it seemed my play-time was ended.

When we went to bed that night I began to talk of home. It was the only way I could save myself from weeping. But Kosi would not listen.

'Be quiet and let me sleep,' he said. 'And get to sleep yourself. You need it. Tomorrow's baking-day.'

'Baking-day?' I asked. 'What's that?'

'You'll see,' he said, and he turned over and went to sleep. I very soon followed him. I had had a long and eventful day and my fatigue was stronger than my sadness.

We were called so early the next morning that it was

still dark. I woke to find Daga, the old lady, a hurricane-lamp in her hand, shaking my shoulder. Kosi was sitting up on his mat rubbing his eyes. When Daga left the room I lay down again.

'No,' said Kosi. 'Come on, get up.' He was putting on his shorts. I did the same and he took me out into the compound and we both washed with cold water from a bucket. Then he led me into an enormous kitchen. The sky was lightening now and the shadowy figures of the old lady and her two assistants – nearly as old as herself – moved about getting great enamel bowls off the shelves, measuring water and salt and flour and palm wine.

'What are we going to do?' I whispered. 'Make bread,' said Kosi.

Then I remembered that I had been told that the old lady was a baker. It had not occurred to me that I should have anything to do with her profession.

She came over to us and inspected our hands and finger-nails. I was sent back to wash mine more carefully When I returned the long table which ran down the centre of the room had been dusted with flour. The two women and Kosi were stationed at intervals along it. I, too, was given a place. Then Daga came and placed before each of us a large lump of dough and she stayed beside me and taught me to knead it. From time to time she came along the line adding more flour to each lump of dough till its consistency satisfied her. By the time we had finished kneading, my back and arms were aching badly. But then came a short rest-time for Kosi and me while the two women oiled the baking-tins with coconut oil and Daga cut up the lumps of dough into different-sized pieces. I learnt afterwards that the smallest pieces were penny loaves, and the others sold for threepence, sixpence or a shilling according to the size. Then we had to put the lumps of dough into the greased tins and line them up neatly on the shelves. I was shocked to see how small the loaves were. Why, they did not nearly fill the tins. The loaves we bought at home were much bigger!

As we left the baking-room the old lady gave us each a large hunk of bread.

'That is for your breakfast,' Kosi told me. 'Daga gives us breakfast for helping her. Don't eat it now, though. We get some tea later.'

When we crossed the yard and went back into the house our master was coming out of his room. I was given his shoes to clean. This job held no difficulties for me because, in order to qualify for a cub badge, I had practised on my father's shoes many times. I sat down and got a fine polish on my master's shoes, not forgetting the back and under the instep. Shoes were important to me. They were a symbol of being grown-up and free. Since that little pair of canvas shoes that my father had bought me when I was four I had never worn any. I often pictured to myself the rows and rows of shoes of every kind that I would have one day. I took my master his shoes. He was sitting in his sitting-room waiting for them.

'A fine polish, Kofi,' he said. 'But you must be quicker in future.'

'Yes, sir,' I answered, remembering to stand up straight.

While I had been polishing, and day-dreaming, Kosi had tidied our master's bed and set the plates on the table for his breakfast. Now I had to watch while Kosi served the meal. I was overawed by the deft way he did it; never getting in the way, never knocking or spilling anything. When the master had finished we poured the rest of his tea into our cups, and drank it, and ate our bread, sitting on a couple of boxes on the veranda.

This was the pattern of our mornings on baking-days, three times a week. On the other days we rose a little later and swept and polished the master's sitting-room and bedroom.

The main part of our day, of course, was spent at school. I was given a shilling on Mondays with which to buy my midday meal for the five schooldays. This was sufficient. For twopence I could buy a good plateful of rice or yam and a little soup or stew. And then there were two pennies left over for an occasional orange or biscuit or sweet. The evening meal we all took in the house.

When I arrived home that first afternoon I found the baking-house once again the scene of great activity. I was called to help but I was surprised when I was told to carry a pile of coconut husks to what looked like a little round hut made of clay. I had noticed it the day before as I sat waiting on the veranda. I thought it looked like a large clay model of an Eskimo's igloo. I wondered whether it was a family shrine like the house of Torgbui Zu in my grandfather's compound. Now I found it was an oven. Coconut husks and firewood were piled in and lit. When all the kindling was burnt the hot ashes were raked out. We were all sent running to the baking-house to bring out the tins of bread on their trays. I was astonished to find that the tins were now full. The pieces of dough had doubled in size.

'What makes the bread grow?' I asked. 'The palm wine,' answered Daga, busily arranging the tins in the oven. 'How does it do it?' I demanded. 'Be quiet,' scolded Daga, 'and bring the bread. Do you want the oven to get cold?'

When all the tins were in, the oven door was shut and sealed.

When it was opened again late in the evening, loaf after loaf of beautiful sweet-smelling bread was brought out. Daga beamed. She gave Kosi and I a penny loaf each. I was delighted. It was hot, straight from the oven, and I had helped to make it. No bread ever tasted so good before. But my eyes grew wet with tears as I ate it. I wanted so much to show it to my mother, and to share it with my brothers and sisters.

Our work was not arduous in the evenings. We had a few errands to run, a few odd jobs to do. If our master had visitors we had to wait on them. But what depressed me was that we were not allowed to go out to play. We had to sit quietly on the veranda ready to answer immediately if we were called. I found this very hard at first, but later I followed Kosi's example and used the time for study.

On Saturdays we washed, starched and pressed our own clothes and our master's, and on Sundays we went to church.

How I pined for the rough and ready life of my own home. The time between afternoon school and the darkness was free for all of us, even my father's boys, except on market-days. We climbed the mountain, played football, raided the fruit trees, quarrelled and shouted.

It was impossible to quarrel with Kosi. At first his confidence and efficiency weighed me down. But he was charming, too, and kind, and after a bit I found myself admiring and copying him.

CHAPTER THIRTEEN

The Path was too Narrow

When I started school in Keta I had a shock. I had been top of my class in Ho. Here, I soon realized, I was near the bottom.

Keta was a big town and the schools were old-established. There had been a full senior school here when my father was a boy. It was the Bishop's see, and catechists and teachers were carefully picked and not often transferred. The school had built up a reputation for steady hard work and excellent results. In other senior schools parents and teachers were satisfied if half the class gained the School Leaving Certificate. Here only one or two boys failed each year. It was quickly borne home upon me that, unless I did something about it, I was going to be one of the rare failures.

About half the boys in my class – Standard 5 – were 'French boys'. These were boys who had been right through school on the other side of the border in French Togo. Having gained their French School Leaving Certificate, they came across the border and repeated the last two or three classes, and got an English School Leaving Certificate as well. They were then equipped to hold a good job on either side of the border. These boys had already done all the work we were doing. They had only to change their language and this was not difficult. They had learned English in their French schools, and had only to become more fluent and colloquial. They were serious and excellent scholars and set a high standard for the school.

I shared a double desk with one of the best of them. After a few days of depression I cheered up and made up my mind to show what I could do. The first thing that attracted me about this boy was his beautiful handwriting, and I practised and practised till mine was almost as good. I found I could still shine at English, and I borrowed books and read and read. My ability at English made it possible for me to get information from text books – a thing which many children could not do – so I read everything I could lay my hands on. This was not very much. It mostly consisted of old text books which my master and teachers lent me from their school and college days. I knew nothing of the joys of story-books. However, all this reading did nothing to improve my arithmetic, and when my father saw my first report he made arrangements for me to have extra arithmetic lessons on Saturday mornings. These classes lasted from about ten o'clock, when I had finished my house-duties, till about two in the afternoon, and were a great trial to me.

By the middle of the year I had settled down to the orderly routine of life in my master's house. The round of household work, school, and evening study went peacefully on, and for some months I fell into no trouble.

It was too good to last however, and before the year was out I fell a victim to the confidence trick.

Kosi went to a different school, because he was not a Catholic, and so I walked to school alone. Every day I passed a group of young men sitting on a veranda. On the ground in the centre of the group was a fairly large square board. It was divided into segments, like a cut cake, each segment numbered and coloured in a different bright colour. In the centre was a pointer, lightly attached. The man in charge turned a handle and the pointer swung round. It came to rest on a certain number, and the winner collected the money which all the players staked.

Every day I stood and watched this game for as long as I dared without being late for school. At first I was fascinated but disgusted. Here was the bad life of the big city about which my father had warned me. Here were young men, whose parents had paid money to send them to school, idling their time away. But as the fascination grew, the disgust vanished. I began to pretend that I had put a penny on a certain number, and to count my imaginary losses, and winnings. Then, one day, I really did put a penny on. Tired of having me staring at them, one of the men said gruffly to me, 'You'd better have a go, boy, if you like it so much.' It was Friday, and I had three pennies in my pocket. Twopence was for my lunch, but the other penny was spare. I put it on number 14. The man in charge smiled and exchanged glances and nods with the other players. A few of them also put pennies on various numbers. The pointer spun, and before my delighted eyes came gently to rest on number 14. The man said, 'Well, well. Beginner's luck, eh?' and handed me sixpence. I was speechless with delight. For sixpence I could buy all kinds of things – a pile of sugarcane, a packet of biscuits, two big sticks of 'chichinga', a box of coloured crayons, a pair of bright ear-rings for my mother, enough sweets for all my little brothers and sisters – it was the largest amount of money with which to do exactly as I liked that I had ever had.

The next week I stopped every morning and put a penny on one of the numbers. One morning I lost my penny, but on every other morning I left the game with sixpence jingling in my pocket and the laughter of the men following me along the street.

On the following Monday our teacher told us that it was time for our quarterly school-fees to be paid. As he usually did, he gave us one week in which to get the money from our parents and guardians. Anyone who had not paid by Friday afternoon, would not be admitted to school on the Monday after. This did not worry me. I went to my master that evening, and he gave me the seven-and-sixpence that my father had sent him some time ago for my school-fees.

In the morning I set out for school, my pocket heavy with the seven-and-sixpence, and the tenpence that was left of my weekly shilling. On the way it occurred to me that if I put more than one penny on the board I should win more than sixpence. I put threepence down on number 13. To find it I took all my money out of my pocket and held it in my open hand while I picked out the three pennies.

'Very rich this morning, aren't you?' asked the man.

'Oh, it's not for me,' I said. 'It's my school-fees.'

Looks and nods were exchanged. The pointer spun and my threepence became one-and-sixpence. Amid laughter and congratulations I put sixpence down – and lost it. Now I wanted to go, but the men persuaded me.

'Come on, now,' they urged me. 'You are mostly lucky. Try again.'

Timidly I put down a penny, but the man refused to spin the wheel.

'Sixpence is the lowest stake this morning,' he announced. His voice had grown unfriendly and I began to be afraid. I put down my sixpence and lost it. Again I wanted to go but one of the men caught hold of me. He took from me all the money that I held in my hand and, two shillings at a time, I watched it go. As the last two shillings was taken I began to cry, 'Give me back my money! give it back! give it back!' But the man in charge lifted me up bodily, and placed me down in the road. 'Get off to school,' he ordered, and gave me a kick that propelled me on my way.

As the morning slowly wore along, the full meaning of what I had done grew clear to me. After registration a few of the boys paid their fees. The fact that I did not was not noticed. Many boys would not bring their money till Thursday or Friday. But I grew cold as I realized that I could never bring mine. At lunch-time I went hungry, and realized that I should go without lunch every day that week.

During the week I made, and rejected, many plans. There was no way I could get out of it without being punished. If I said I had lost the money I should be punished for carelessness. If I said it had been stolen from my desk there would be a big inquiry and perhaps the whole truth would come out. And, whatever happened, the incident would be reported by my master or teacher to my father. The whole week passed slowly on, and I grew tired from hunger and worry and sleeplessness. On Friday afternoon the teacher read out a list of half a dozen names, mine among them. 'These boys,' he said, 'will not be admitted to school on Monday unless they bring their fees with them.' I had only two days left in which to solve my problem.

On Saturday morning I went as usual to my extra arithmetic lesson. I was slower than ever that day. My teacher asked if I were sick, but I said no, so he kept me at it till about three o'clock. As I walked home I passed the landing-stage from which the canoes left to cross the lagoon. There was a single canoe there, with half a dozen people in it, and the boatman was looking round for more passengers. Suddenly I made up my mind what to do. I would go home and tell my father how I had lost the money. If I told my master he would punish me, and I would still have to go to father and be punished again by him before I could get the school-fees replaced. This way I at least faced only one beating. I told the boatman I wished to go with him. He asked for sixpence. I told him I had no money, and that I was going home to ask my father for my school-fees. As I spoke I began to weep about it for the first time. I told him I would not be able to go to school on Monday if I could not get my fees. He looked at me for a moment, then he patted my shoulder, and said, 'Get in, boy.'

It was four o'clock by the time we had enough passengers to start, and the wind had dropped. The boatmen had to use their poles the whole way across the lagoon. The journey seemed endless to me. I was still a little nervous of the water, and I was very cold. Before we were half-way across I was regretting the impulse that had started me off on the journey to face my father, and I had realized that I would be in trouble when I returned for running away without permission. When we reached the landing-stage at Anyako the brief tropical twilight had already begun. In ten minutes it would be dark. All the people hurried off the boat to reach their houses before dark. But I had nowhere to stay in Anyako. There were five miles of dark and deserted road between Anyako and Abor. There was no question of my walking along it until the morning. No one in his senses went out at night if he were a stranger in the place. My father and grandfather had told me that when a chief died someone had to be killed, in order that the chief might have company on the way to the next world. In the old days one of his family or servants might offer himself for this death. At other times a criminal or prisoner under sentence of execution might be available. But now, under foreign rule, these things were forbidden. So the death of a chief would be kept a close secret, and his elders would send a group of young men out in the night, to capture and kill any stranger whose disappearance would not be noticed or reported for a considerable time. Here I was the perfect victim. No one knew me, no one knew where I was. My master would imagine me safe at Abor. My father thought me safe at Keta. How did I know that the chief of Anyako or of one of the villages near by had not recently died?

For a long time I stood on a dark corner watching the last of the travellers hurry home. In an hour the place was deserted. Everyone was safe at home but me. Everyone had a light and a fire and food and friends but me. The market was near and I lay down on a bench under a palm-branch shelter. But I could not sleep.

Hunger and fear combined to make me shiver, although the night was really warm. A new fear came to me. My father gave to his house-boys another reason for not being out at night. 'Boys and men who roam about at night are not often on any innocent errand,' he said. 'If you are seen out at night you must not be surprised if people think you are a thief.'

Now I was old enough to be regarded with suspicion. I racked my brains again and came to a decision. Just then a woman passed, walking briskly and carrying a lantern. I went towards her, trying not to startle her.

'Please,' I said, as politely as I could, 'will you tell me the way to the house of the Head Christian?'

She looked at me suspiciously, holding up the lantern so that the light fell on my face.

'Which Head Christian?' she asked.

'The Head Christian of the Catholic Church,' I answered. Still she was not satisfied.

'Who are you?' she demanded.

'I am Kofi, the son of Nani, the headmaster of Abor.'

'What are you doing, out in the night at Anyako?'

'I am on my way home. I go to school in Keta. But the canoe was so slow that it was dark when I reached here. I want to ask the Head Christian if I may sleep in his house.'

Then she was friendly. 'Come,' she said. 'I also am a Catholic. I will show you the way. Step carefully, there are big puddles.' She took me to the house, and even knocked on the door for me, and waited till it opened before she went away. I told my story again to the Head Christian and was kindly received. 'You are lucky,' he said. 'The priest has just arrived. He is going to say Mass

133

for us tomorrow. That is why the household is still up so late.'

He called his wife to bring me food. It was something I particularly disliked but I was so hungry that I ate it and enjoyed it. For a few hours some of my fears were removed, and others were not yet upon me. I was given a mat and a place to sleep. But I did not sleep very well. I was still cold. Anyako is an island, joined to the mainland by a causeway, and the wind blew off the lagoon all night.

I got up early in the morning and offended the kind Head Christian by refusing to stay for Mass. Missing Mass on a Sunday without a very good reason is a sin for a Catholic. I knew this but somehow I felt that I had got so deep in sin now that nothing would help me. I only wanted to get home to my mother.

I ran most of the five miles to Abor and when I arrived at the house no one was there. The whole family and household had gone to church. I rested and waited for them. My mother and the children arrived soon. My father was out visiting the sick and the absentees as was his custom.

'Kofi! What has happened?' my mother cried when she saw me.

'Nothing, Mother,' I answered. 'I wanted to come home for the week-end and see you all. But my teacher kept me late at my arithmetic lesson, and then there was no wind and the canoe took a long time to get across the lagoon. So I stayed the night with the Head Christian at Anyako.'

'You were a sensible boy,' she praised me. 'But how will you get back tonight?' 'I will stay till tomorrow morning. It is market-day and there will be plenty of canoes.' 'Well, that will be nice for me,' said my mother doubtfully, 'but your father will not like it.'

'You tell him for me,' I pleaded.

Not long afterwards my father came home. When I heard his heavy footsteps I ran into the bedroom. From there I listened to my mother talking to him.

'Kofi is here,' she said.

'Is something wrong?' my father asked.

'No, he just wanted to see us,' my mother told him. She explained why I had not arrived the day before. It did not occur to either of them that I had come without my master's permission.

'How will he get back tonight,' my father asked.

My mother told him my answer to that question. Then my father called me. 'Had you any special reason for coming home?' my father asked me. Now was my chance to explain and get it over. But I had no courage. While I had been away I had remembered the good things about my life at home and forgotten my fear of my father. But now, standing before him, I was more afraid than ever. He looked so big. I remembered the way his questions always probed out the truth from me, however carefully I tried to hide it. My mother, and my little brothers and sisters, and the house-boys and -girls were all standing round. How could I make my confession and be questioned and broken down in front of them?

'No, Papa,' I answered, and the moment was lost.

'Is there no school tomorrow?' he asked.

'Yes, there is school,' I said.

'Then somehow you must return today,' said my father. 'You must leave here directly after lunch. Is that clear?'

'Yes, Papa,' I answered, but I knew I could not go.

After lunch my mother gave me a new cloth, and sixpence for my fare on the canoe. But I did not go. My mother was perplexed. She could not force me out of of the house, and she could not bring herself to denounce me to my father. I slept in a corner of the boys' bedroom, and no one spoke to me for fear of drawing my father's attention to my presence.

In the morning I covered my head and face with my cloth and lay still.

I heard my father speak to my mother as he sat down to breakfast. 'Well,' he said genially. 'Did Kofi get off all right?'

My mother did not answer. There was a long silence.

'Yawo!' my father called and my young brother answered, 'Papa!'

'Where is your brother?'

'He is in bed.'

'Is he sick?' my father asked.

'Perhaps he is,' my mother put it hastily.

'You know Kofi never stays in bed if he can help it.'

'Tell your brother to come here,' my father told Yawo.

'Papa wants you,' he said. But he need not have spoken. I had heard every word.

I went with dragging footsteps and stood before my father. He put his heavy hand on my forehead.

'He is perfectly cool,' he said. Everybody was very still and quiet.

'Now, Kofi,' said my father. 'You will tell me why you do not want to go to school today.'

'Please, Papa,' I said. 'I cannot go to school today, because I have not paid my fees.'

'What's this?' said my astonished father. 'But I sent your school-fees to your master weeks ago. Did he not give them to your teacher?'

'No, papa,' I answered, strictly truthful. Suddenly, to my surprise, it seemed to be all over.

'There is some misunderstanding somewhere,' he said impatiently. 'But I am in a hurry, this morning. Look, here is the seven-and-sixpence. Hurry off now. You will be in time for afternoon school. Pay your fees, and I will sort it out with your master when I next see him.'

In a minute he was gone, leaving me shaken with relief, and with seven-and-sixpence in my hand. I rushed around tying my clothes into a bundle, and putting on the new cloth my mother had given me – it was quicker than dressing in shorts and shirt. I embraced my mother and rushed out of the house. I had run and whistled for a mile or more along the road, before it dawned upon me that my troubles were far from over.

There was a big stone on the roadside at the place where this thought came to me, and I sat down on it as my legs grew weaker under me. I had told my father that my master had not paid my fees; my father would see my master about it; my master would tell him that he had given the fees to me. I had only postponed the inquiry and the inevitable consequences. And to my crime of gambling my fees away, I had added the crimes of running away without permission, missing Mass on Sunday, and lying to my father. For a moment I could see no solution at all. I wanted to run into the bush and die. Then an idea began to grow in my head. Such a daring idea that I felt as if I had received a challenge. I dared myself to carry it through. I needed two lots of school-fees. One with which to pay my teacher, and the other with which to pay back my father. I had one lot in the corner of my cloth. Very well, I would get the other.

I tore off a strip of my new cloth and hid it, with the money wrapped in it, under the big stone. I tied a knot in a clump of long grass near by. Then I began to run home. I ran as fast as I could, driving myself on, so that I was covered in sweat and fighting for breath. I put on a last effort as I reached the gate of the house and collapsed at my mother's feet.

'Kofi! Kofi!' she cried, kneeling beside me and wiping the sweat from my face. 'What happened? Are you hurt? What is it?'

The house-girls and the little children who did not go to school crowded round. I tried to speak, but was so agitated and breathless that I only gasped. 'Bring cold water,' called my mother, and she splashed it on my face. I began to enjoy my act, and gasped a bit more and rolled up my eyes. But her next order took away some of my fun. 'Go and fetch the master, quickly,' she told her maid.

I struggled up, 'No, mama, I am all right,' I protested. But I was too late. The girl had rushed off, only too delighted to be the bearer of such exciting news.

Still gasping, and trying to squeeze out a few tears, I told my mother that I had been attacked by thieves, and my money taken from me, and that only by running with all my might had I escaped being murdered. My audience was entirely convinced. My mother hugged me tightly, and the girls and boys bombarded me with questions, and exclaimed with horror when I showed my torn cloth. In the middle of all this my father walked in. For once his appearance did not make anyone quiet. My mother at once began to abuse him for forcing me to go that morning.

'The gods are with children,' she said. 'The spirits told him that he should stay late in bed this morning and go in peace. But you forced him to go quickly, without his bath or his breakfast. And look what has happened! He was set on by thieves, and beaten and robbed!' My mother, carried away, began to improve upon my account. 'Look!' she cried. 'He is almost dying.' Here I rolled my eyes again, and then closed them and sank back against the wall. I was only too glad to shut out the sight of my father, who was obviously not impressed, and who had brought with him his long cane. But my mother had not yet become aware that he was not moved by her speech. 'Look!' she cried again. 'See how they have torn his new cloth! See how he tried to keep the money, so that they had to tear off the corner in which it was tied!'

She stopped for breath, and a horrible sound made me open my eyes. My father laughed!

'Edzi,' he asked. 'Do you believe this story?'

A look of utter surprise came over my mother's face. 'What else can it be?' she asked.

'Why do you allow your own son to deceive you?' he asked her, rather wearily. 'How can you believe this fantastic story? Would thieves set upon a small boy with no luggage? How could they know he had any money? Do thieves make open attacks in broad daylight on market-day? Are there any cuts or bruises on the boy? No, Edzi, use your brains. Kofi wanted to take a day off from school for some reason of his own. That was quite clear from the beginning. If you allow him to get away with things like this, it will not be many years before he will sell the house from over your head without your knowing anything about it.'

All the excitement had died down. There was no doubt that my father had, with his few reasonable words, stolen my audience's support from me. I glanced round carefully from under my lashes.

My mother's face still wore the look of surprise, but it was fading into doubt and annoyance. The house-girls' expressions were openly amused. Only my small brothers and sisters still looked at me admiringly.

My father spoke to me for the first time. 'Stand up, Kofi,' he ordered.

I stood up, uncomfortably aware that his grip had shifted on the cane.

'I do not know why you are playing this game,' he told me. 'And, at the moment, I am too busy to find out. You will leave this house immediately, and get back to Keta as quickly as you can. Probably by now, most of the canoes have left. You must do the best you can, and make your own apologies to your master and your teacher. But I tell you this, Kofi, if I find out that you have disobeyed me, you will never, as long as you live, forget this day or cease to regret it.'

This threat, which everyone knew he would not hesitate to carry out, made all further conversation impossible. Amid complete silence I walked out of the house and, as I set off once again on the road to Anyako, I heard my father's footsteps turn out of the gate and hurry back to his school.

Once out of sight of the house, I walked slowly, watching closely for my clump of knotted grass and my big stone. I sat down on it, and pretended to be resting till there was no one on the road. Then I safely retrieved my money. But I did not get up and go. My thoughts were too hopeless. I was still in the same position about my fees, but I had piled up still more crimes to be held against me. How I wished I had told my father everything yesterday morning. The whole incident would be closed by now. I should be sitting in my desk at school, my fees paid, and my apologies made to my master. Apart from being a bit sore about the hands or seat, I should be enjoying life as usual!

As I sat brooding over my troubles a child's voice shouted, 'Kofi! Kofi!' and my little sister came running round the bend of the road. I could hardly believe my eyes. She was only six years old, and we were a mile away from home.

'What are you doing here?' I asked her.

'What will Mama say?'

'Mama sent me,' she panted proudly, 'to give you this.' She gave me a small closed tin. I opened it and inside were eight shillings. I stood and stared at it. Then I looked at my little sister. And a great wave of shame came over me. I knew myself clearly for the first time, and despised myself. All my thoughts were different now, and even harder to bear than the previous ones had been.

My father had given me good advice about bad company and gambling, and I had been too stupid to heed him. I had lost my father's money, but I had been too cowardly to tell him so. I had caused my master, who was always kind to me, unnecessary anxiety by rushing off home. I had deceived and perplexed my mother by my childish act. I imagined her now, not knowing what to believe, and yet understanding that for some reason I was desperately anxious to have another seven-and-sixpence.

'Well,' said my little sister in a down-to-earth-voice. 'I must go back now.' I shut up the tin and realized another worry that I had caused my mother. She would never normally have sent such a little child on such an errand. But she knew that the house-girls would talk about it and betray both her and me.

'What would you have done,' I asked my sister, 'if I had walked fast and not sat down to rest?'

'I was to go on till I found you, even if it was at Anyako,' she told me. 'Mama said so. She said it was very important, and the good spirits would go with me and look after me.' I took her hand.

'Come,' I said. 'I will walk back again with you to make sure you are safe. Only you must never tell anyone but Mama, or Papa will beat me.'

'It's a secret,' she said, and as far as I know she has never mentioned it again.

I took her almost home. Then, for the third time, I set out for Keta. All the canoes had left with market produce long before I reached Anyako. With some idea of not wasting any more of the money my father was spending on my education, I went to the senior school there and asked permission to join the class for the afternoon. In the evening I went again to the Head Christian and tried to be especially polite and helpful. I was on the first canoe that left as dawn was breaking the following morning, and a good wind carried us to Keta in record time. My master had not yet left for his office. Now my resolution faltered a bit as I stammered my apologies and explanations. Even then I could not make myself confess the whole truth. I said I had lost the money, and had been afraid to say so, and had run home to ask my mother for more.

My master said little. He looked at me closely and made a few quiet remarks. Just as I thought it was all over, Daga came out of the bakehouse.

'Is that all you are going to say to the boy?' she asked angrily. 'His father warned you that he needed a strong hand. Are you not going to punish him?' 'I have no doubt that his father has done all that is necessary,' said my master, dryly, and went away to his office. I hurriedly changed into my clean uniform, that Kosi must have pressed for me, and ran to school. Here I had more explanations and apologies to make and again I could not tell all the truth. I said I had had to go to my father at Abor to get the fees. There was no trouble.

I tried to concentrate on my lessons, but I was still weighed down by this new feeling of shame which I had experienced.

In the afternoon the headmaster sent for me. With him, in the office, was one of my father's friends. 'This gentleman has come to inquire whether you have returned safely from your father's home,' the headmaster told me. 'He is returning to Abor tomorrow. Perhaps you would like to send some message to your family?'

'Yes, please,' I said eagerly. I took seven-and-sixpence from my pocket. 'Please tell Papa,' I asked the man, 'that I was mistaken about my school-fees. My master had them and they have been paid. So I do not need this money that he gave me. Please give it back to him. And please tell my mother I thank her for her present.'

I felt so happy. At last everything was cleared up. No, not everything. My mother's money was not repaid. It was my mother who had paid my school fees that term. I laughed and ran on my way home. I would get the best report I had ever had, and when I took it home next holidays, I would pointedly present it to my mother instead of to my father. It would be amusing to watch her expression and see if she understood why I had done it.

CHAPTER FOURTEEN

My First Girl Friend and Her Friends

The second year that I spent with my master at Keta was also to be the last. But, at the time, nobody knew this and I felt very settled and content. My home life was ordered and pleasant; I was neither spoilt nor ill-treated; food was sufficient, and rest adequate. At school I was reasonably successful and popular; I had a good teacher and was very interested in my studies. The mischief I fell into was mild, and just served to break the monotony of my otherwise blameless life. The punishments that came my way were only sufficient to keep my feet on the narrow path.

This year was a time of peace before the storms that surrounded me during my last year at school; a smooth run before the obstacle race that was before me. And I shall always be grateful for that peaceful year. During it I managed to acquire enough ability at my lessons to enable me to keep up with my class during the following year, when, for much of the time, trouble made studying impossible. Not that my days were entirely without adventure – that, I think, would not be possible in the life of a boy. Strangely enough, since I was not really interested in girls at this time, most of my difficulties arose because I felt it was necessary to have a girl friend.

I was thirteen and it seemed to me that all boys of my age had a girl friend. I felt I ought to have one, but perhaps the memory of Tona still lingered with me, because I found none to attract me. Besides, I did not meet many girls. The school was for boys only. The corresponding girls' school was run by white nuns and was known as the Convent. Most of the pupils were boarders, and the few day-girls carefully avoided the boys. Daga's servants were nearly as old as herself, and I was not allowed to go out to play, and to roam round the countryside, as the other boys were. So my meetings with girls were few indeed, and for some months I gave it little thought. Then I became a member of the school band. I was a side-drummer. The band was a very important part of the school and I was very proud to join it. The first time I wore my uniform – it was royal blue with a great deal of gold braid about it – was for the Empire Day celebrations. In Keta the festivities were even more imposing than they had been in Ho, and I was completely happy, until I noticed that the uniform with which I had been issued was not complete. Every other boy wore, tucked into the band of his shorts, and cascading down at the side, a bright silk handkerchief. I went to the senior band-boy who had issued my uniform. 'I haven't been given one of those handkerchiefs,' I complained. He grinned, 'Too bad,' he said, 'who should have given you one?' 'You, I suppose,' I answered. 'No, not me,' he laughed. The rest of the band was laughing now. 'Well, how can I get one?' I asked bewildered. 'Grow up, small boy!' answered the leader, while the other band-boys hooted with mirth.

I discovered later that the boys' girl friends gave them the handkerchiefs. I made up my mind that, before the next big day, I too would have a handkerchief. But first, of course, I had to have a girl friend, and I eventually met her in the night-market.

My master's house was on the edge of the town and bordered onto the Hausa quarters. The Hausa people, being not only of a different tribe but also of a different religion, do not mix very much with my people. They build their own settlements on the outskirts of towns. Between my master's house and the Hausa quarters were a cinema and a night-market. Kosi and I, of course, were not allowed to go to the cinema, but we were not forbidden, on hot nights, to take our stools and sit in the gateway of the house. From there we could see the arrival and departure of the cinema-goers; we could see the lights and hear the cries of the traders; and our evenings were sometimes enlivened by a quarrel, or even a fight, between those who had spent too much in palm-wine bars.

Occasionally one of us was sent to the night-market to buy something. This happened seldom, for Daga was a careful housekeeper, and bought all her supplies herself, with due deliberation, in the day-time. But if my master had unexpected visitors he would send one of us for cigarettes or matches. And, now and then, Daga ran out of kerosene and sent us to buy a bottle. This was my fault. It was one of my duties to light the fire in the morning and to heat water for my master's bath, and to boil a kettle for his tea. Often I got up a few minutes late, and sometimes the firewood was wet, or the wind in the wrong direction. When this happened, and I could not get the fire to burn quickly and brightly, I stole kerosene out of Daga's lamp, and poured it on my smouldering firewood. Then, in the evening, when Daga came to light her lamp, she would find it empty. She suspected me, but she never openly accused me or set any trap for me. Perhaps she remembered the days when she was a little maid-servant in someone else's house, and a dull fire and late bath-water could be a cause of trouble and tears. Anyway, she just shook her head when she found her lamp empty and sent me to buy a bottle of kerosene at the night-market.

One night I found that the kerosene was being sold by a girl of my own age. She attracted my attention at once by her quietness in the middle of so much noise and bustle. She sat still on a stool, with her bottles of kerosene stacked in a shallow, enamel bowl at her side. She did not call out as the other traders did, and I thought, when I went closer, that she looked a little frightened. There were plenty of other girls as young as her, and younger, hawking their wares in the market, but they were bold, noisy girls. My mother would at once have said they were bad girls. Girls of good families were not normally to be found in such a place at such a time. I bought my bottle of kerosene and opened conversation. 'I've never seen you here before.' I spoke in English, partly to show off, but mostly to find out if she went to school. She answered in the same language. 'My mother is sick. She could not go to market at all today. I said I would sell this for her.'

'Where do you go to school?' I asked. 'At the Convent. I'm in Standard 5.' 'I'm in Standard 6,' I told her, glad to be her senior. She smiled and I saw that she was pretty. 'I know,' she said, 'I often see you going to school. I know your name too, and where you live.'

I was surprised and pleasantly thrilled. It was obvious that she was interested in me.

'What else do you know about me,' I prompted her.

'I know you are in the school-band,' she said. 'I saw you on Empire Day.'

This reminded me of my need to get a silk handkerchief and therefore to have a girl friend. Here was one who must already have noticed the fault in my uniform, and whose friends would tell her what her duty was in this matter.

'Are you anyone's girl friend,' I asked her. She shook her head. 'Then what about being mine?' I suggested. She hung her head and did not reply, but that was good enough for me.

I returned home whistling, and Daga's scolding because I had been so long slipped off me like water off a duck's back.

My new girl friend was called Rose – all the Convent girls were called by their baptismal names, not by their African day-names as most of us were. She altered her route to and from school so that we could walk together part of the way. Gradually, she and I became friendly with two more couples, boys from my school, and girls from hers. We took our walks in a group, and then none of us could get into trouble with parents, teachers or guardians. But it soon became apparent that, to one couple, these meetings meant something different from the casual friendship experienced by the others. Kwami and Mary were a little older than the rest of us and they were soon in love. While Rose, Agnes,

Kobla and I were quite happy to meet in a group, Mary and Kwami took every opportunity to slip away from us.

In October the Catholic Church, to which we all belonged, held a regular evening service, and we were all expected to attend. I easily got permission from my master, and the others from their parents, and every evening the six of us walked along the beach to church and back again. On moonlight nights the walk was beautiful. The silver-tipped waves rolled on to the silver sand, and the dark coconut trees dipped and swayed above us. We were all affected by the scene, and by the emotional hymns we had been singing. We split up into pairs. Rose and I sat on the beach and held hands a little, but on the whole we preferred throwing stones into the sea, or racing to the nearest coconut tree. And it was the same for Kobla and Agnes. But Mary and Kwami went right away from us, and after a while we tired of waiting for them, and we went home. This happened on a good many occasions, and eventually some rumour reached my master's ear, for he called me and questioned me. 'Who do you walk to church with, Kofi?' he asked me.

'With some of my friends,' I answered cautiously.

'Well, let's have their names,' he prompted me. His method of questioning me was much less frightening than my father's, and I generally told him the truth because I felt he deserved it. But his leniency made it possible for me to reserve part of the truth from him when I felt it was expedient.

'Kwami and Kobla,' I told him.

'Yes,' he said, 'and what about the girls?' Obviously he knew, so there was no point in lying to him.

'Mary, and Agnes, and Rose,' I said.

'All Convent girls?'

'Yes, sir.'

'And do you all walk together, all the time?'

I realized the point of the questions now and so my line was clear.

'Yes, sir.'

'You all walk together, all the way to church, and all the way back?'

'Yes, sir.'

'Have you and your girl – which is she, Rose? – ever walked apart from the others?'

'No, sir.'

'Have Kwami and Mary ever gone away from you?'

'No, sir,' I answered firmly, hoping that he had no real evidence to the contrary.

He repeated his question, asking me if I were sure my answer was truthful. I said it was, and he dismissed me.

The next day the six of us compared notes. We had all been questioned, and had all, with the quick cunning of children used to trouble, made the same replies.

Someone had seen a boy and girl embracing on the beach, and had told Mary's mother that the girl looked like Mary.

We all decided that this was too dangerous, and gave up our walks together. But I knew from Kwami that he and Mary met secretly every day.

Kwami was the boy I most admired in the class. He was one of the 'French' boys, and imitating him had done much to improve me in every way. One of the most wonderful things about him in my opinion was the fact that he lived alone. He rented a room in the town. Each weekend he crossed the border, and visited his family in Lome, and returned with money and provisions for the next week. He confided in me, and told me of his love for Mary. I could not imagine loving a girl in the way he described but, because of my love for Kwami, I became almost as anxious as he that she should be kind to him. I was worried every morning, until I saw by his face that their evening meeting had successfully taken place. But I did not like Mary. My preference was always for quiet, gentle girls, and I thought Mary bold and loud and hard. I felt instinctively that she would hurt Kwami, and it was not many weeks before I was proved right.

After two or three occasions when Mary did not turn up at the appointed meeting-place, Kwami discovered that she was spending her time instead with a young man of the town. I was soon able to confirm this, as I saw her, on one occasion, going to the cinema with her new boy friend. He was flashily dressed in American clothes, and obviously had money to spare, and a way with girls. Quiet, serious Kwami was no match for him. When I told him what I had seen, I was shocked by the stricken look on his face. I could not understand that it was possible to care for a girl like that. As the days passed, he gradually went to pieces. It was obvious that he was not eating or sleeping properly. His work in class was bad, his appearance careless. He told me that he was resorting to magic to win Mary back. This really upset me. My father's training, and my close association with the Catholic Church, had not made me disbelieve in magic. That was impossible, for it was woven closely into the lives of all my people. But I had become afraid of taking part in it. The priests told us that all magic was of the devil, and a terrible punishment awaited those Catholic children who had anything to do with it. So I feared, not only for my friend's health and sanity, but also for his soul. And all because of a wretched girl.

I decided that Mary ought to be punished, and that I would see to it.

I gathered my friends together and enlisted their help. There were eight of us and we finally agreed on a plan. One evening after school we waylaid Mary on a lonely footpath, along which she passed as she went home. Three times we had to let her pass because she was accompanied by a friend, but on the fourth she was alone. As she came along I was idly kicking a ball about, but as she got into range I stopped the ball, and kicked it viciously right at her. It hit her as I had meant it to do, and she cried out. This was a signal to my companions, and with wild howls they leapt out from the bushes where they had been hiding and surrounded her. Each of them had something to throw. Those who did not possess a ball had brought a hard, unripe orange. And now we played a vicious game with Mary. Keeping her imprisoned in our circle, we bombarded her with our balls. Backwards and forwards she ran, trying to get out of the circle, but every space closed up before her, and every few seconds she was hit again by a ball, or an orange, thrown by an angry boy. My gang got too excited, and began to get out of hand. They closed in on the terrified girl and began to pinch and slap her. I called a halt to the punishment, and made them let her go. As I watched her stumble away, dishevelled and weeping, I felt content with my vengeance.

But the next day I was not so sure that I had been clever. As we stood in our lines in the school-compound,

153

waiting to march into school, we were all dumbfounded to see Mary and a grim, white-robed, white-faced nun cross the compound, and enter the headmaster's office. I exchanged anxious glances with my friends. The word was given and we all marched into school. The first two lessons crept by, and nothing happened. Surely Mary and the nun must be gone by now. They couldn't be in the headmaster's office all this time. But no one had seen the voluminous white robes flapping back across the compound.

As the bell for recreation rang, and we all sighed with relief, the headmaster entered the classroom. He was closely followed by Mary and the nun. This was the first time I had seen a white woman at close quarters, and her cold blue eyes, and thin pale mouth, revolted me.

'Now, Mary,' said the headmaster. 'Please point to the boys concerned.'

To us he said, 'If this girl points to you, stand up.'

One by one Mary pointed out all those who had taken part in tormenting her. She hesitated once or twice, but in the end she made no mistake. I suppose she knew us all fairly well, and if she wasn't sure, she could make a good guess at those who would be likely to support me. When asked to indicate the leader, she pointed to me without hesitation.

I put on a bewildered expression, and my friends followed my example. We were led into the headmaster's office to be questioned.

'So you boys waylaid this girl yesterday evening, and beat her,' he said.

There were bewildered and outraged cries of, 'No, sir!' and 'It wasn't us, sir!'

'Are you telling me that this girl is a liar?' asked the headmaster. I think he was not too pleased to have the school invaded by women! Especially women with a complaint. He seemed unusually willing to listen to us. We all spoke again in an offended chorus. 'She must be, sir, if she says that.' 'It must have been some other boys, sir.'

'Be quiet, all of you,' he snapped. 'Kofi, the girl says you were the leader. What have you to say?'

'Nothing, sir,' I answered. 'I don't know anything about it.'

'She says you threw balls at her,' he told me.

I let the light dawn slowly over my face, as if his words had made me remember something. 'Oh, sir,' I said. 'I think I know what she is talking about. No one beat her, sir. My friends and I were playing with a ball on the way home, and the ball accidentally hit her.'

'Accidentally?' queried the headmaster.

'Yes, sir,' I said, and there were murmurs of agreement from the other boys.

'And then,' I went on, 'Mary started to shout at us and abuse us.'

'Then you beat her, I suppose,' suggested the headmaster.

'No, sir,' I insisted. 'No one beat her. Some of us answered her back. But we wanted to get on with our game. So we told her to get off home.'

The other boys had got the idea now. 'Yes, sir,' put in one of them. 'She kept on abusing us, and she was in the way, so we pretended to chase her to make her go.'

'Yes, sir,' said another. 'She walked right into the middle of our game anyway, or else she wouldn't have got hit.'

'Who kicked the ball that hit her?' asked the headmaster.

The boys all looked at me, waiting for a lead.

'I'm not sure, sir,' I said. 'It might have been me. The game was pretty fast just then, sir.'

I looked questioningly round at the other boys. Several of them made doubtful excuses.

'It might have been me, sir.'

'I didn't see, sir.'

The headmaster looked round at the nun. 'Well, Sister,' he said, 'I think perhaps your young lady has been exaggerating. The boys' story sounds more likely than the girl's.'

Mary began to cry with frustration and rage. We tried not to look too smug.

The nun tightened her thin, tight lips and stood up.

'I believe the girl,' she said. 'It is your duty to punish these hooligans.'

She walked out of the office, and out of the school, without a backward glance, Mary trailing behind her.

When she had gone the headmaster took out his pen and silently wrote down all our names. We began to feel worried.

'I have no doubt that you have been doing something to bring discredit to the school,' he said. 'I am equally sure that I shall not learn the truth from you. So I do not propose to waste any more time on the matter. I shall consider later how to punish you.'

He dismissed us, and sent us back to the classroom. By now we felt anything but smug.

The days wore on. A whole week passed and the matter was not mentioned. On one occasion we saw the headmaster hold a short conversation with our class-teacher, who listened carefully and nodded his head. A piece of paper passed between them, both consulting it from time to time. Later that day I was tidying the teacher's table and I recognized the piece of paper. It was a list of our eight names. But still nothing happened, and we forgot about the matter. Mary kept out of the way, and Kwami recovered his spirits.

Then, one by one, my companions got into trouble. Kobla talked in class and was sent to report himself to the headmaster. We learnt with indignation that he had received eight strokes of the cane. Such a big punishment for such a small crime! Other people talked in class that day and were simply rebuked. Another boy in our gang forgot to do his homework, and a third was late for school. When both of them were sent to the headmaster, and were given eight strokes, we began to realize what was happening. Our clever headmaster knew that we were guilty, and was not going to let us get away with it. But he was not going to be dictated to in his own school by a woman, and a white woman at that. So he had decided on this way of settling all scores, confident that we should see his point. We did, and we gave him our grudging admiration. Still, we intended to beat him if we could. The remaining five of us turned into angels. We were polite, punctual, industrious, quiet. Our teacher had a hard time to catch us out in a fault. But, one by one, my friends made a mistake and paid the penalty. In the end the last ones were relieved when their turn came. The strain was too great. At last they were all free to be their natural selves but me. I got reckless. I had to get it over. I stopped making any special effort. But good luck dogged me. I could not get reported.

The weeks went by. The school concert occupied all our thoughts. This was a great affair to which the whole town came. Before our parents and friends we sang songs, acted plays, and displayed all our talents and abilities. This year I was to be the star turn, for I could play the piano. I had inherited my father's love of music, and before I left home he had taught me to play the church harmonium. Now the school had been given a piano, a beautiful thing, all the way from Germany. The Standard 7 teacher was a musician, and he soon found the feeling I had for music. He taught me to play, and gave me many happy hours. Now I was to play at the concert. I practised and practised, and was very happy. All thought of the trouble about Mary had passed from my mind.

On the morning of the concert our class-teacher was busy, with a chosen group, decorating the hall. The rest of us were given some work to do on our own. None of us bothered much about this. We knew it was only a formality. No one really worked on the day of the school concert. From time to time the headmaster emerged from his office to restore us to order. On one of these occasions he caught me a long way away from my own desk. He ordered me to go to his office. I waited nervously. By the time he came the closing-bell had rung, and the school was waiting for him to address and dismiss them. He wrote a note and gave it to me. He directed me to take it to his deputy, the Standard 7 teacher, who was sitting in his empty classroom. The headmaster watched me all the way from his office to the classroom. I had no chance to run away, or to read the note.

I handed it to the teacher. He began to read and then

he looked up with a troubled frown. 'The headmaster says I am to beat you, Kofi,' he told me. 'What have you been doing?'

'Only fooling about in the classroom, sir,' I answered.

'But he says I am to give you eight strokes,' he went on. 'You must have been doing something more than that.'

I was silent. I did not know how to explain that justice had caught up with me at last.

But there was more to the note and the teacher read on.

'So it's that business about the girl,' he said to himself. Then to me, 'Tell me, Kofi, as one music-lover to another, what happened that day?'

'We did throw balls at her,' I said.

'What on earth for?'

'Because she jilted one of my friends,' I cried. 'And went out with a rotter from the town.'

He smiled a little. 'And everyone else concerned has already been caned, I understand.'

'Yes, sir.'

'And now it is your turn.'

'Yes, sir,' I said. My voice was shaking and I knew I was trembling. I had never got over my fear of being beaten.

The teacher still sat still.

Then he got up, and shut the door and window that looked on to the compound where the assembled school was chanting its prayers.

'It would be a pity to spoil the show tonight,' he remarked.

Then he set his leather briefcase on the chair and took his cane from the cupboard.

He glanced at me standing in complete bewilderment.

'You'd better make a bit of noise,' he said. The quiet voices went on chanting outside. The teacher raised his cane and hit his briefcase a resounding smack eight times.

'You'd better go out of the other gate,' he said to me. 'You don't look upset enough. And remember, Kofi, not a word about this, even to your best friend. I don't approve of your taking vengeance into your own hands, you know. I am only concerned that you should do me credit at the piano tonight.'

And I did.

CHAPTER FIFTEEN

The Family Reunited

'Good-bye, good-bye,' I called to Kosi and Kwami. The boatman pushed off, the canoe glided through the water, and I was on my way home for the holidays. I had not been home for a year and I was happy, excited and confident. I brought with me a good report and several prizes, which would earn my father's praise. I knew that I had learned how to behave in a considerate way, and to be helpful in the house, and I was determined to let my mother see the results of my training. I had a boxful of presents, some made with my own hands, some bought with money saved by going without lunch, for my little brothers and sisters. I was quite sure of my welcome at home. And I had something to talk to my father about, something which I felt sure would make him happy. I had decided that I wanted to be a teacher. I don't know when this desire became obvious to me. It was no sudden revelation. I suppose it was in my blood, and my position as eldest of the family had given me an early interest in the ways of little children. Now I knew enough, about myself, to know that I had the abilities I needed. I was what I later learned at college to call 'an all-round person'. I was sufficiently good academically to pass the examinations; I was interested in games and sports, and played in the school-teams; I had my music, and had lately found a lot of pleasure in trying to paint. I would use all these interests in teaching. I wanted my father's permission to sit next year for the Entrance Examination to a Teacher Training College. I knew that money would be a difficulty but I believed I might get a scholarship.

I felt grown-up, almost a different person from the silly little boy who had gone home last year. I squirmed a little in my seat, as I thought of all the scrapes that little boy had got into, and the worry he had been to his parents. I thought that now I understood my father better. I even gave him the benefit of the doubt, and tried to persuade myself that he did not realize how hard he hit. Or perhaps I had an extra thin skin! Anyway those days were gone. I was nearly fourteen, and in another year I would be finished with school. I was confident that my father would see that I had changed, and that a new relationship was before us.

He was not in the house when I arrived. My reunion with my mother and the children was as happy as I had hoped. My mother exclaimed at how much I had grown, and how well I looked; my ten-year-old brother began to follow me around and fetch and carry for me; my smallest sister insisted on riding everywhere on my shoulders. Only when my father came was reality less pleasant than my imaginings. He nodded his head when he looked at the report and prizes that I so eagerly showed him, but he did not attempt to talk to me. He went silently into his sitting-room and closed the door. Returning to my mother I noticed that she looked worried.

'Is something the matter, Mama?' I asked.

'Your father has been transferred again,' she told me.

This was indeed a tragedy. All my parents' savings had gone into the house they had built here at Abor, and my father had been assured that he would remain here. After the wrench of leaving his fine school at Ho, he had not found it easy to show the same energy and devotion to the school here. But he had done it. The school was progressing nicely, and my mother had managed to do a little trading. They were just beginning to find life a little less hard, and now they were to move again.

'Where are we going?' I asked.

'Back home,' answered my mother, 'to the school where your father started.'

I brightened. I thought this was good news. 'But won't you and Papa like that, Mother? You will be with all our family and friends.'

'It is the house,' she explained. 'I don't know where we shall live.'

Just then my father emerged from his sitting-room, and looked at me in his stern way. At once all my confidence evaporated. I was furious with myself because I was afraid, and then furious with him for making me so. After all, I was doing nothing wrong. Why did I feel guilty just because my father looked at me. My mother looked a little guilty, too. She stopped talking to me and began to bustle about. Perhaps he disapproved of our discussing his affairs – but they were our affairs, too. Perhaps he disliked seeing me sitting down doing nothing. I got up and walked out of the house, uncomfortably aware that I should have asked his permission, and that my walk, which I was trying hard to make natural, was stiff and jerky. I felt his eyes burning holes in my back. I knew that I should never talk to him about being a teacher.

Bit by bit, over the next fortnight I learned the extent to which this transfer would alter our lives. Since there was no house for us at home, and my father had no money to build one, the natural thing for us to do was to go back to my grandfather's big family house. This was the traditional African thing to do. My father and his family had a right to shelter there. But in practice the idea was not pleasant. The house was already more than full with my fishermen uncles and their wives and children. Between them and my father there were many disagreements. He thought them uneducated, they thought him proud; they were pagans, he a Christian; they were polygamists, he a firm and outspoken advocate of monogamy.

He was well aware of how unpleasant life would be for him in the family house. It was a terrible blow to his pride to have to go and ask his father for house-room.

My mother flatly refused to live in the paternal house. She knew she could not live a day with my uncle's wives without quarrelling. She had another idea. Her mother lived at Keta, only three miles away from my father's new school, and only a few yards from the school I attended. She proposed that we should all live there, and that my father should cycle to school. This seemed to me a good idea, but my father would not hear of it.

'Live in my mother-in-law's house,' he cried in horror. 'Oh, no! Not me! If I cannot be master in my own house, I prefer to obey my own father than my mother-in-law.'

'Then we shall have to part,' said my mother. 'For I will never live in your family house. You will go there, and the children and I will go to my mother.'

My father seized on the one weapon he had to force my mother to obey him.

'If you go to your mother's house you go alone,' he said. 'The children go with me.'

'That is impossible,' argued my mother, impatiently. 'Who would look after them?'

'There are women in my father's house,' he pointed out.

'No one cares properly for children but their own mother. You have often said that husband, wife and children should live together as a family, and that parents should bring up their own children without interference from relatives,' Edzi reminded him.

'It is true,' said my father. 'I believe it. You are forcing me to go against my beliefs.'

'Master,' pleaded my mother, 'let the children come to Keta with me. Truly, I cannot live in your father's house. You know in your heart, that it would be too difficult for us all. And the children are too young to be parted from me. They will live with me at Keta. They can all go to good schools there. And you will come often and visit us. It is the best solution – you know it is.'

Neither my mother nor I had any doubt that my father would agree to this sensible suggestion.

But we had underrated his pride. He could not bear to be under obligation to his mother-in-law. And he wanted his wife to obey him.

'The children will come with me,' he repeated in his

cold hard voice. 'If you want to see them you will have to come to my father's house. I shall not allow them to visit you while you insist on separating yourself from me.'

My mother was frightened. She knew that he meant it. Although she sat quite still and did not speak, her distress was so great that I could feel it. I dimly understood the terrible cruelty of using a woman's love, for her children to force her to do something she could not bear. In an effort to comfort her I made the silliest mistake of my life. If I had kept silent I might have spared us all much unhappiness. But I said, 'Mama, I shall be living in Keta, too. I will come and see you often. My master will let me come every day.'

My father saw his hold over my mother slightly weakened.

'You will not be living in Keta,' he said to me. 'You will live in your grandfather's house with me.'

'Papa, no!' I cried. 'I have another year to do at school.'

'You can walk to school. It will not hurt you.'

'But you sent me to my master. He expects me to stay with him another year.'

'You left my house only because there was no suitable school for you,' my father reminded me. 'Now circumstances have changed. It is no longer necessary for you to be away from your own family. I shall write to your master today and tell him you will not return.'

Still, in my anger, I rushed in where angels might well have feared to tread.

'I shall come and see you every day, Mama,' I told her. 'I shall come at lunch-time.'

My father took my shoulder in his heavy grip and

turned me to face him. For a moment my anger enabled me to glare defiantly back at him. Then I lowered my my eyes and was afraid.

He spoke very quietly and he meant every word he said.

'You will live in your grandfather's house, and you will walk into Keta every day, to school. While you are in Keta you will not visit your mother. If you see her in the street or any other place you will not stop and speak to her. Those are my orders. If you disobey them I shall certainly get to know. Perhaps,' he added, 'you imagine that you are now too old to be punished. If so, you are mistaken. If you disobey me you will find this out.'

There was nothing more for any of us to say. My mother went to Keta, weeping as she said good-bye to us. My father, and I, and the children, went to the family house. There was still a week of the holidays left.

My grandmother was overjoyed to see us and gave us a tremendous welcome. She had not seen us since we went to Ho, when I was about seven years old, and my sister and brother were babies. The three little ones she had never seen at all. She brought us food, and water to wash, and did all she could to make us comfortable. I began to think that life here would not be too bad.

The first difficulty came when we were shown where we should sleep. My grandfather had only been able to spare one room for us. This became almost entirely filled with our luggage so that there was only room for my father's bed. I was to sleep on the veranda outside this room; the younger children were found places with aunts and cousins. The little ones, who had never been parted from my mother before, wept when bedtime came. I had promised my mother that I would keep the youngest one with me, and I tried to, but my aunts insisted that it was not good that such a little girl should sleep in the open. They took her, crying, away. I appealed to my father, but he upheld my aunts, though I do not think he was any happier than I.

But we had all had a tiring day, and the little ones were soon asleep. My father sat on the veranda for half an hour. I sat on the steps beside him and longed to speak to him, but I did not know what to say. When he went into his room I lay down on my mat and tried to sleep. But I was not used to sleeping in the open and the night-sounds kept me alert. The moon was bright and from where I lay I could see the whole compound. My grandfather's house was really a series of small houses built round a large sandy quadrangle. The houses were not all of a pattern; some were made of concrete and some of swish; some were big and some were small; some had well-made doors and painted window-shutters, others had simply door and window holes. I do not know how the rooms were allocated to their occupants, but, as some were obviously nicer than others, I imagined their allocation might be the cause of much discontent. I noticed that the room my father had been given was one of the best, and I wondered who had been turned out to make room for him. In the centre of the compound was the well which supplied the whole family with water, and here and there were the rough shelters under which the women cooked. The whole place was permeated with the smell of fish, the source of my grandfather's wealth. The house of his gods, too, was there – Torgbui Zu's house, and the house of the big net. Before both were dishes of palm-oil and food that my grandfather had put there. My grandfather's own house was some way away. He and my grandmother slept there, and spent their leisure hours there, and entertained their guests there, but for much of the day they were among their children and grandchildren supervising the life of the big house. I heard a dog growl in his sleep, the moon went behind a cloud, and I too slept.

In the morning the house woke early. Before dawn the adolescent boys and girls got up and drew water, and swept the verandas, and rolled up their sleeping mats. Then the men and women emerged. The men called for water to wash, and then went out in the first light, carrying the nets. The women lit the cooking-fires, and warmed water to bathe the children, and made porridge to feed them. I too rolled up my mat, and swept the veranda, and brought water to my father, and tidied his room. As soon as they awoke, my little brothers and sisters ran to me, and I started clumsily to dress them. But my aunts came and laughed at my efforts, and bathed and dressed the children. This time the children were willing to go with them, and in a few days they were happily absorbed into the life of the big house. I felt that, in being happy, they had betrayed my mother, and I made several attempts to keep them to myself, but I could not help admitting to myself that I was glad to be free of the responsibility of them.

I did not settle down so easily. I discovered to my own surprise that I had become fastidious. I did not enjoy eating with the other boys from a common dish, and the strong-smelling fish that figured in almost every meal made me feel sick. I several times made my grandmother angry by eating very little. She said, quite rightly, that my mother would say that she was not looking after me properly. I found, too, that my life with my master had made me value orderliness and quietness. Here there were neither. The members of the family came and went, ate and slept, wherever it pleased them. Mealtimes were irregular, and noise was continuous. My father solved this problem by spending most of his time out of the house. He did not realize that it was a problem for me, too. The hours I spent reading in my father's room gave my cousins the impression that I was proud and unfriendly.

For these reasons I looked forward to the re-opening of school, when I too would be out of the house all day. But for another reason I dreaded it. When school re-opened I had to decide whether I would visit my mother or not. I was convinced that I ought to, and yet I was afraid of the consequences. I was sure that my father was wrong to forbid it, and yet I had been trained to regard obedience as the highest virtue and duty. There seemed to me no clear solution, indeed, I did not even know what I wanted to do. I bore both my mother and father a grudge for putting me in this dilemma.

So the days went by, and at last the time came when I first set out on my three-mile walk to school.

CHAPTER SIXTEEN

Still Narrower

I was tremendously glad to be back at school. I was in the top class – a real senior – I had a teacher I liked, and my best friend was elected form prefect. I was in the school-band and the school-football team. I had a girl friend who was pretty, good-natured, and not too demanding. Life was good. For a few days I forgot my worry about my mother. I left the house early, and returned to it late. The only thing that troubled me was that I was always hungry. My father gave me money for my lunch, and imagined that I had breakfast and supper from my grandmother. But the truth was that breakfast was always late, and I had to leave the house before it was ready; and in the evenings, when I was tired, I could not eat the strong-smelling and oily stew which my cousins enjoyed.

One day I was surprised to receive a message from my mother asking me to go and see her. I was at once both conscience-stricken and afraid. I went to the house and as soon as I entered the room my mother began to weep. I realized that she had been parted from her children for two weeks, and had had no news of them. She had relied on my promises, and I had deserted her.

'Mama, Mama!' I cried. 'Please don't be so unhappy. Everything is all right. The children are quite all right. They like it there.'

To my surprise this turned out to be the wrong thing to say.

'You see,' she cried. 'Those wicked women are stealing my children from me. And your father agrees to it. They will give them sweets and make them forget me.'

'But, Mama,' I said. 'Don't you want them to be happy? Aren't you pleased that the aunts treat them well?'

'Oh!' she said bitterly, anger drying her tears. 'It is only at first they treat them well. Soon they will get tired of them. They have their own children. In a week they will be neglecting mine. Anyway,' she went on, 'I do not believe they keep them clean and neat like I do. Do they now?'

I thought, and had to admit that, after the first few days, my little sisters and brothers had played about the compound naked, as their cousins did. At first this had bothered me, but then, seeing them happy, and being immersed in my own anxious thoughts, I had not worried about it. Now that my mother pressed me, I remembered too, that bathing was not the serious daily ritual that it was in my own home. The older children splashed in the sea; the little ones were captured by an aunt and bathed just when there was water and time to spare, or when the child looked extra dirty. My sympathies swayed back to my mother. In the last year I had grown to realize the importance of cleanliness. One of my prizes had been for hygiene. I had even, I suspect now, become a bit of a dandy. I remember rubbing powdered chalk on my handkerchief and dusting my face when I thought my skin looked too shiny! I began to agree with my mother that the children were not being properly cared for.

She went on to ask me about their food. Here, speaking for myself, I told her the food was not very nice. My mother dried her eyes and looked at me piercingly. 'Yes,' she said. 'You are thin. Are you hungry?'

I admitted that I was.

'Come after school,' she told me, 'and I will have something ready for you.'

'Mama, I dare not,' I said. 'You know what Papa said.'

'Well, come at lunch-time tomorrow, and I will make you a big lunch. Then you can spend your lunch-money on something to eat on the way home.'

The idea was too tempting. I fell easily. Soon I was going every day to lunch. While I was at my mother's house, too, I had a hot bath each day, and I left my clothes with her to be washed and mended and pressed. I was not happy about it, but I could not resist it. She was comforted by seeing me fed and clean, but still she grieved for her other children. She asked me to take them food, but I did not dare. They were not hungry, they had got used to the different food, but I could not make her believe this. She became more and more upset. I conceived the idea that I should go to my grandmother, and ask her to intercede for my mother. But she was a proud old lady, too. She had little love for my mother, regarding her as undutiful and full of new-fangled ideas. Besides, I could not do anything without risking my father finding out that I had been disobeying him.

While I worried, and thought about this, the blow fell. My father heard from an acquaintance that I regularly visited my mother.

He called me and asked me if I had been to see my mother, warning me at the same time that there was no point in my lying to him. I admitted it, and was beaten. I was hurt, not only by the cane, but by the knowledge that some of my rough and ready cousins would be pleased to see me punished. They considered that I needed taking down a peg or two. I cried with anger as well as with pain, and lost control of myself, and shouted at my father, 'I shall visit my mother whenever I like! You have no right to stop me!'

As soon as I had spoken I realized with horror what I had done. I had openly defied my father before a number of witnesses. I knew he would never give in now until he had subdued me. And I discovered in myself a pride like his. I also could never give in.

Every day I went to visit my mother, but the food tasted like sawdust in my mouth. Every evening my father asked me if I had been, and I told him I had, and he beat me. After a few days I knew he dreaded asking me, just as much as I dreaded replying, but neither of us would give in. I became sick at the sight of food, and super-sensitive to pain. Every day I invented some awful thing and tried to make myself believe it, so that I would not cry out when my father beat me. One day I told myself that if I cried the baby would fall into the well and drown; another day that I would fail my School Leaving Examination. My grandparents intervened, but my father merely took me to the school-office to punish me.

Both he and I knew that something had to happen to stop this, but neither of us could give in. My mother noticed that I was becoming thin and ill, and no longer enjoyed her cooking, but I did not tell her what it was, and she blamed my grandmother for not looking after me.

One lunch-time, when I was sitting in my mother's house, my father himself walked in. He came to rebuke her for allowing me to disobey him.

At once there was a terrible quarrel. All the pent-up feelings of both of them burst out. She cursed him for taking her children from her, for starving me and beating me. He blamed the whole thing, including my wickedness, on her. I could not bear it. I stopped my ears, and ran out of the house, back to school.

That evening my father said nothing to me, but the tension was like the heaviness of the atmosphere before a storm. How I envied my young brothers and sisters who took refuge with the aunts and were protected. I slept little that night. I wondered if I should slip away and go back to my master and beg his help. But, although he was kind, he was rather cold and correct. I did not think that he would interfere in such an affair. I felt alone and friendless in the middle of so many people.

In the morning I took refuge in a book that my teacher had lent me. I had been reading a particularly thrilling chapter when darkness fell the night before and I wanted to finish it. But reading for pleasure was a thing which no one else in the house, not even my father, did, and was counted as one of my lazy habits. My grandmother called me to breakfast, and I answered her, but did not go immediately. She called again impatiently, and my father came to the door of his room and looked at me angrily. Everyone was strained and short-tempered. I went to my grandmother, but I kept my book in my hand, with my finger to mark the place. Perhaps I was ill-mannered in the way I took the plate, and thanked her for it. I sat down by the well and began to eat, but I did not like the food, and when I looked at it closely there were a few dead ants in it. Furtively, I dug a hole in the sand with my toes, and dropped the food into it, and covered it up. Then I returned the plate to my grandmother who began to express her pleasure that, for once, I had eaten a good meal.

But I was unlucky. A small cousin, hearing me praised, piped shrilly, 'He didn't eat it! He buried it by the well.'

My grandmother went to the well and soon saw that the accusation was true. She began to weep, 'Oh, Kofi,' she said, 'what am I to do? Your mother believes I starve you. You are getting thinner every day. I tried to make you happy. I tried hard. But you will not eat. What more can I do?'

My father heard her and came to the door of his room. He called me, and I crossed the compound, and went up the three steps on to the veranda. As soon as I stood before him, the book still in my hand, his temper snapped. He slapped my face, on both sides, till my head rocked dizzily backwards and forwards. Then, while I stood dazed, he went into his room and returned with his cane. I turned to run, but he caught hold of my wrist with a grip like a vice. I fought and twisted, while he rained blows all over my body. I just could not free myself, and in the end I fell and crouched on the ground, one arm dragged up by my father's grip, the other protecting my head. I was wearing only my shorts and the cane fell again and again across my bare shoulders.

My grandmother screamed, and hurled abuse at my father. She came to stop him, and as she pulled at his shirt, I made a final desperate effort to free myself. Something seemed to twist and give way in my wrist, and I was free. I stumbled and fell down the steps, and across the compound, to the big gate. I fumbled with the latch, whimpering with fright and pain when I found I could not use my hand. Someone came and unfastened the gate for me – a little girl – a sister or a cousin – I don't know.

Out of the house at last, I ran all the three miles to my mother at Keta. Without consciously thinking about it, I took the back ways, the lesser used paths, and few people saw me.

My mother bathed my wounds, and put me to bed, weeping louder than I, and cursing my father. I wished I had not come to her. I wanted to be alone and in the end I begged my mother to leave me. I thought that I should never recover from this humiliation, and I wanted to kill myself. But I fell asleep from exhaustion, and when I awoke I was calmer. Then black hatred came to fill my heart, and I decided to kill my father. I became feverish, and my head ached so much that it eclipsed the pains in my wrist and back. Then I thought that I was dying, and I was glad, and got pleasure out of the thought of my father's remorse, and the bad things his family and neighbours would think of him.

But, of course, I did not die. Neither did I kill my father. After a few days he came to see me. Evidently my parents and grandparents had had earnest discussions about the whole situation. They had decided that we must all live together again. My father had then bought a piece of land, and on it he proposed to build a little house made of plaited palm branches, until he could afford a better one. A house of coconut-palm screens was a poor man's house, and I knew that both my mother and my father must have hated having to come to this decision. But they both blamed themselves, as well as each other, for the near-tragedy that had come to us. They were humbled by the thought which my grandparents had put before them, that my father might, in his temper, have done me some lasting damage. And so, as soon as possible, we were to have our own home again.

I went to sleep peacefully that night. The dreaded meeting with my father was over, and though he spoke little I knew that, in spite of everything, we did not hate each other.

That was the last time he beat me, and from that time he began to be an old man, and before I was twenty-four he was dead. I never achieved that father-and-son relationship with him that I so dearly wanted, and my brother, who pleased him more than I, was still only a child when our father died.

Epilogue

There is little more to tell about my boyhood.

The coconut-mat house was quickly erected, for the whole family worked at it. The boys cut the great branches and carried them home; the girls tore the leaves in strips and laid them in the sun to dry; the women plaited the strips into screens; and the men nailed the screens on to the framework they had erected. As we worked we talked and laughed and quarrelled and sang. Our bare feet loved the soft white sand that was blown from the beach and which covered the ground on which our house was built. The breeze brought the smell of the sea to us, and when we stopped to rest in the evening we could watch the little fishing-vessels coming home.

It should have been a pleasant time, and for the younger children, it was. But I shared my parents' view that this house – this shelter – was not fit for a teacher and his family. This was the kind of house that poor and illiterate men lived in. Like my father, I blamed the

Mission authorities for the way in which they had transferred him here and there to suit their own convenience, without giving any thought to his. Seeds of bitterness against the church were sown then, although they did not grow for many years.

When the house was finished, and the sandy compound entirely surrounded by a high reed fence, my parents and their children moved in. Once more we had a home and, poor as it was, it was better than the separation that preceded it. We left our more precious, and less-often-used, belongings in my grandfather's house, because the coconut-mat house could not be secured against thieves. We cooked in the open and most of the family went to bed with the sun, because fires and lamps and candles were too dangerous. The walls of our house were bone dry, and one spark from a fire would have sent the whole thing up in flames.

But I was in my last year at school. I could not afford to spend the evenings in sleep or story-telling. I had to study, and to study I had to have light. So I spent most of my time in the house of my friend Koku – that same boy with whom I had gone to buy my first pair of shoes. He and I really studied hard, and we were often joined by other boys from the class. Koku's father put aside a room for our use, and my father gave us all his textbooks.

We had to pass in three subjects in order to get our School Leaving Certificate – in English, arithmetic and general subjects. General subjects was a mixture of history, geography, nature study, hygiene and civics. English and general subjects did not bother me unduly, but arithmetic did – very much. The paper was composed partly of mechanical arithmetic and partly of 'problems'. Our teaching had been so theoretical that I had never realized that 'problems' were examples of real-life situations in which arithmetic was used. To me they were entirely incomprehensible. But I discovered that it was possible to get a pass mark on the mechanical section alone if every sum were right. So I deliberately gave up trying to understand 'problems' and set to work to cultivate speed, neatness and accuracy. No one queried the wisdom of this. I do not think our teachers at that time were altogether at home with 'problems' either!

Every Friday, we had a mock examination in those subjects, and the names of those who achieved a pass-mark were posted on the school notice-board. How we worked, and what agonies we suffered over these results! It is hardly possible to understand nowadays what that examination meant to us. In many cases the boys' parents had made real sacrifices to send them to school and to keep them there so long. Some of the boys had walked long distances to school; some had struggled against the pangs of hunger as they tried to work on one meal a day; others fell asleep in class because they had been up till midnight selling in the night market; the unluckiest ones were punished regularly for being late although they had been at work since five o'clock on the family farm, or in some other way helping with the work of the household. For some of the boys, schooling had been interrupted many times when funds were low, or extra hands were needed on the farms or at the nets. Others had suffered the humiliation of being sent away because their school-fees were long overdue, or their clothing was inadequate; and others again had done the best they could without the necessary text-books.

Now the day of reckoning was almost here. This one day decided whether so much sacrifice and so much endeavour had been in vain. Even the lucky ones, like myself, whose schooling had caused little hardship either to themselves or to their families, were just as anxious. We had no excuse for failing. In our case we came from the families of teachers, and if we failed our shame would be greater than that of our classmates.

The great day came and went. Even the weeks of waiting for the results went at last, and thirty-four out of the forty of us had passed. We were congratulated and feasted wherever we went.

Our certificates were presented to us one Sunday morning at the end of Mass. School and church were part of one another in those days. The Mission built and financed the schools, and trained and directed the teachers. The schools existed firstly to provide and instruct converts for the church, and secondly to provide teachers, and clerks in government offices. The curriculum was designed to those ends. But to us it was 'education' and the only way to become a 'big man' in the new world.

The church was packed. People stood in the aisles, and gathered outside every window and doorway. Scores of people who had no hope of seeing what was happening inside the church waited in the churchyard to congratulate us when we came out.

One by one our names were called and we walked through the crowded congregation to receive our certificates. My parents had lent me a kente, and for the first time I wore it over one shoulder as the men do, instead of tied at the back of the neck as the boys do. I was small for my age and the kente was full-sized and

I could hardly manage it. I came back clutching and stumbling through the smiles of my family and friends, but nothing could spoil the occasion for me. I pictured my father in years to come exhorting my little brothers and sisters to 'do as well as Kofi has done'. I did not know that my father's early death would leave me responsible for the education of the younger ones.

When we had all received our certificates we walked in a procession to the school where another ceremony of praise and congratulation was held.

My parents gave a party for myself and my cousin and my father's younger brother. We were all in the same class and we had all got our certificates. I remember that the main dish was roast chicken and rice, and that the largest helpings and the choicest bits of meat were given to us. I expect the same kind of feasting went on in the homes of all the successful thirty-four that day. What happened to the other six I did not ask. In my youthful cruelty I never gave them a thought.

In spite of my School Leaving Certificate my future was not quite settled. I still wanted to be a teacher, and I had sat for and passed an examination to a teacher training college. But my father was required to sign a bond before I could actually be given a place in college. He had to guarantee that I would teach for at least five years after the end of my training, and he would forfeit a large sum of money if I failed to keep this agreement. He still regarded me as unreliable and troublesome, and he was not really willing to stake so much on my good behaviour.

Those were anxious days for me, and I prayed a great deal. St Anthony of Padua was a favourite saint with us schoolboys. My friends reported that he had a good record on such matters, so I prayed to him.

Whether it was St Anthony's doing, or whether it was the pressure brought to bear upon my father by my mother and my teachers, I cannot say, but the bond was signed in the end and my future arranged.

The college was 200 miles away, and it seemed to my mother that I was going to the end of the earth. We all rose at dawn on the day of my leaving. My mother filled a calabash with water and sprinkled corn-dough into it. She raised it to the east and to the west, and she invoked all the family gods, and asked that they would protect me on my journey, guard and guide me while I was away, and bring me safely home. I looked round at the bowed heads of my brothers and sisters, heard the soft whimper of the newest baby from my mother's bedroom, and the tears rolled down my cheeks.

The prayer finished, my father led me out of the house, the little coconut-mat house which I had so despised but which held all the people that I loved. My father himself accompanied me to the main road, my mother's maid-servants following with my boxes on their heads. When we had gone a few yards we looked back and saw my mother also following. My father shouted at her angrily, because she was the mother of a new baby and it was against our custom that she should expose herself to the early morning dew. She turned back, weeping.

We did not wait long by the roadside before a lorry came which would take me on the first part of my journey. My trunks were lifted on and I climbed up beside them. Once settled I turned to bid my father good-bye, and saw the hardest thing in all that desolate parting. There were tears in my father's eyes.